LAUREL-LEAF BOOKS

In a nightmare you sometimes get a feeling: This can't be true. You tell yourself it's a dream. In the best nightmares you know it's a dream and you relax. You don't exactly enjoy the terror, but there's comfort in knowing that you'll wake up in the morning.

But there are nightmares that take you through the horror and drive it home, until you wake up, not in the morning but in the dark of the night, sweating, trembling, wondering who and where you are. For a few moments you stare into blood-red dark that slowly turns black again. A familiar room comes into focus as the dream recedes. But the horror stays.

And there are nightmares of a different kind. Bad dreams that are part of reality. That *are* reality.

PATRICIA WINDSOR is the author of several highly acclaimed books for young readers, including *The Summer Before*, an American Library Association Best Book for Young Adults, and *Killing Time*, both available in Dell Laurel-Leaf editions. She lives near New York City.

ALSO AVAILABLE IN LAUREL-LEAF BOOKS:

Patricia Windsor

THE SANDMAN'S EYES

LAUREL-LEAF BOOKS bring together under a single imprint outstanding works of fiction and nonfiction particularly suitable for young adult readers, both in and out of the classroom. Charles F. Reasoner, Professor Emeritus of Children's Literature and Reading, New York University, is consultant to this series.

Published by
Dell Publishing Co., Inc.
1 Dag Hammarskjold Plaza
New York, New York 10017

Laurel-Leaf Library ® TM 766734, Dell Publishing Co., Inc.

ISBN: 0-440-97585-9

RL: 5.1

Reprinted by arrangement with Delacorte Press

Printed in the United States of America

April 1987

10 9 8 7 6 5 4 3 2 1

WFH

To my parents,
Bernhard and Antoinette Seelinger, with love.

"A dangerous crossing, a dangerous wayfaring, a dangerous looking-back. . . ."

THUS SPAKE ZARATHUSTRA,
Friedrich Nietzsche

THE
SANDMAN'S
EYES

PART

I

1

I had come back from being away a long time. I stepped off the train, put my suitcase down, and looked at the town. It looked the same as when I left. The big iron Kornkill sign still hung crazily from one hinge and the red neon letters still spelled BUD in the window of the Station Diner. Even the smell of the place was the same: a sour tang from Krackmayer's sausage factory mingling with the brooding river's fishiness. I was home.

Rosie and my grandfather started to argue about taking a taxi from the station. Grandpop wanted to take a bus to save money but Rosie was determined to take a taxi. Maybe she wanted to smuggle me up to the house, so no one would know that Michael Thorn was back in town. I felt a sudden squeeze in my chest and I knew it wasn't homecoming joy. It was fear.

One of the town taxi drivers, slouching against the fender of his black cab, caught my eye and gave a knowing smile. I looked away. I remembered he was called Suds and he had once yelled at me for falling off my bike near the parkway. I was a little kid then; Suds probably didn't remember, but I hoped my grandfather would win the argument and we would take the bus.

But Rosie won. She beckoned to Suds and he threw down his cigarette and hitched himself into the cab. We piled into the backseat, trying to be polite and casual at the same time, unsure of who should be first or last in the door.

I got stuck between Rosie and Grandpop and it was a strange feeling, their bodies so close, pressing against me like bags of old clothes. At the school, where I'd been all this time, everybody smelled the same: steamed and flattened by the school laundry, baked in carbolic soap. Rosie and Grandpop smelled real, like people who could choose their own brands of toothpaste and soap and decide whether to use them or not. Freedom, I thought, was as simple as that. Suds revved up and we careened out of the parking lot.

The taxi chugged up Kornkill's skinny Main Street and I would have been content to sit and stare straight ahead, but Rosie started talking like a tour guide. She pointed out the old stores that had been boarded up and the new stores that had been put into place, garish and modern, like glittery scars. I saw I was wrong to think the town was the same.

Pandolphi's shoe repair had been transformed into a gourmet cheese shop. I thought of old Pandolphi and how he used to talk through a mouthful of nails. I wondered where he was now. I wondered how he felt about his shelves full of cheese instead of shoes.

"Look at that," Rosie said, poking me in the ribs. "Pasek's grocery is gone, too."

"What does the boy care," my grandfather snapped. He was busy keeping his eye on the taxi meter, calculating the price of the ride.

But I did look, because I remembered Pasek's was where Lindsay and I used to stop before we went down to the river. We'd buy her favorite picnic: Twinkies, Cokes, Chipwiches, or cherry ice pops that turned our teeth red. I thought of Lindsay and wished I hadn't. Thinking of her gave me the same gut-ache I used to get from our picnics. I wished Rosie would shut up and stop pointing out historic landmarks that weren't even there.

My last trip down Main Street had been in a police car. I'd kept thinking I was seeing the street for the last time. I didn't believe them when they said I was being taken to a special school. I had conjured up bloodthirsty visions of punishments I felt sure they had planned: hanged by the neck until dead, gassed in the nose, shot in the heart, electrocuted into oblivion. I was steeled for death. But instead of death they gave me the green room.

"Why don't you stop your harping?" my grandfather was saying to Rosie. "It's Mickey's first day home. You can go to the supermarket in the mall, so save your breath."

Rosie drew her coat around her shoulders and stared out the window. Her eyes had been scared as a rabbit's for a moment, as if she was afraid of the new stores. She always took the bus downtown to shop on Main Street and now she'd have to go someplace else.

All of a sudden, because of Rosie's fear, I felt as if a big weight had rolled off my chest. I could learn to drive and take Rosie shopping in the mall. I owed Rosie. She had come to see me every month for two years. My grandfather had never come, not once, except today to pick me up, and that was only because they wouldn't release me unless he did. I don't know if I loved Rosie, who was Grandpop's wife and not my real grandmother, but I felt something. And I felt good that I had something to plan for. But even as I was feeling good, hugging my plans to me as a kind of security blanket, another part of me was smirking. *Just like Dr. Kline and Dr. Painter, the medical vaudeville team, they said you gotta have a goal. Fixate on your goal, you dip, and do everything by the book, and you are going to be one hundred percent fine.*

This smirking part of me is something I acquired at the school. It's like a running commentary on my emotions. It always wants to show me the other side of the story. It always wants to stick in its cynical opinion. Maybe now that I was home, I would have to get rid of it.

Never mind. I put the idea of learning to drive in a special place in my brain to save for later. I felt better. Things might be all right. Then we came to the top of Main Street where it crosses Monrovia Boulevard and the taxi stopped at the intersection for the light.

Monrovia Boulevard runs north and south like

the river. It climbs into woods that smell of pine and mulch, where the black iron gates of the cemetery seem to rise higher than the trees, where Lindsay once told me you could catch death from walking barefoot on the graves. And it drops down to the sausage factory and railroad yards, and to the black iron gates of Monrovia Park. I didn't want to look at Monrovia Park. I turned my face north to the woods and waited for the light to change.

Then I felt the jerk of the cab and the tilt of a turn. Rosie gave a little gasp.

"There's a barricade," she said. "It wasn't there yesterday."

"Nothing to worry about," Suds said. "We go around the detour. Won't cost a penny more."

I shut my eyes. I felt Rosie's hand on my knee and I wanted to grab it and squeeze it, but I didn't dare.

I tried to remember the names of the streets and where we could turn to get back to Carhart Street, but my heart was pounding and getting in the way of my mind. I felt so helpless and stupid with this fear and yet I couldn't get it to stop. I knew Suds must be looking at me in his mirror. He was probably thinking: That Thorn boy came back, he's just as daft as ever.

Then Rosie's grip relaxed and we were turned again. I opened my eyes slowly and found myself looking at the brown shutters of No. 5 Carhart Street. We had arrived. And while my eyes had been shut, we had passed Lindsay's house. Coming home from anywhere at all had always meant passing Lindsay's house first. But this time I'd missed it and it was like an omen. I wanted to ask about the barricade, but Grandpop was pushing us out of the taxi, anxious to pay the fare and try to get away without giving a tip.

Suds leaped out to open the doors. He grabbed my suitcase off the front seat. "Here, you can take this, sonny," he said. "You can handle this, can't you?"

I heard his patronizing words, but I was too busy to be bothered to answer. I was busy making myself believe I was really standing on Carhart Street, that in front of me was really home. It looked smaller than I remembered. The porch needed a coat of paint. Who had raked the leaves and done the small repairs in the two years I was gone?

Suddenly, everything seemed too sharp-edged and poignant: the nip of winter in the air, the rustle of fallen leaves, the smallest pressure of a pebble under my shoe.

"What's the matter, cat got your tongue?" Suds asked, and laughed.

"He can talk fine," Grandpop rushed to say.

Rosie glared a warning. She didn't like hanging her wash out in front of strangers, as she called it.

"Give it to me," I said, and took the suitcase from his hand.

Funny words for a homecoming.

Rosie had the door key ready, it dangled on a chain with a plastic flower. We walked like a parade up the front steps: Rosie, me, Grandfather. When the door opened, everything looked strange and familiar at the same time.

"Well, you're home," Grandpop said.

"Yes, he is," Rosie said.

I took a step inside.

Home. That word. It was supposed to mean so much.

I heard the faint strains of a violin. But when I turned, I saw it was my grandfather making the sound, trying to mask the beginning of a wail. Bright tears brimmed and glistened.

"I'm sorry," I said, astonished that the pain I'd thought was only inside myself had somehow escaped into my grandfather's pale blue eyes.

"What's to be sorry?" he said, digging into his pocket for a handkerchief. He laughed at himself as he swiped at the tears. "Take off your coat. What are you waiting for, an invitation?"

Rosie tried to cover up the moment with her chatter. We bumped into each other at the closet door, just like we had bumped each other getting into the taxi.

"I'll make coffee," Rosie said. "We need to warm up."

Me, I felt roasting hot already. I had prepared myself for all kinds of problems in coming home but I hadn't thought of this embarrassment. Ordinary small things, they seemed the hardest and the worst.

"Your room's waiting," my grandfather said in

a gentle voice I didn't recognize. "Same as you left it; only cleaner."

I couldn't get used to this new grandfather-of-jokes; it was disconcerting. I longed for a typical scolding or some unreasonable request, so I could get angry, feel normal again.

As if reading my thoughts, he put away his hanky and his smile.

"It takes a little time to grow familiar again," he said. "Pretty soon you'll forget you were ever away at all."

2

That train journey to the school two years ago had been a nightmare. They'd shot me full of tranquilizers but I got hallucinations instead of calm nerves. I felt as if strips of my flesh were tearing away with every jolt of the train. I sat and watched Kornkill melt against the sky. In the setting sun the river was the color of blood.

There was no use mentioning hallucinations to anyone. Their response to every request, including permission to go to the bathroom, was "Shut up!" So I suffered quietly, like one of those martyrs Rosie was always telling me about, holding my body together piece by piece; keeping guts, heart, kidneys, intact by sheer force of will. Night fell. The train sped on to the school.

I concentrated on the arrival. At the school, I believed, there would be an infirmary and I would be taken there. I formed a picture of this infirmary in my mind and it became so real, I could see the gleaming white fixtures, the neat beds with blinding sheets, the starched nurses and sympathetic doctors. But wishful thinking has nothing to do with reality.

I was dragged off the train and thrown into another car. No one spoke to me. We traveled through darkness and I saw nothing but a wall of black. The headlights slashed the wall like lasers and we managed to push through, inch by inch, until we came to a gate. By this time strobe lights were going off at the sides of my eyes. "Get out," they said, and I stumbled into a rock courtyard.

My bladder was bursting, my stomach gurgling with acid, my eyes doing tricks like the Fourth of July, but the infirmary kept me going. Soon everything would be all right.

But they took me to a big bathroom and told me to wash up and then they put me in a room and left me there. Nobody came to take care of me, to see if I was alive and in one piece. I had a vision of myself falling apart, eyeballs rolling into corners, arms and legs dropping off like discarded clothes. I felt scared. This can't be true, I told myself, it's just a bad trip from the drugs.

After a long while I realized I had a choice. I could let go and forget Michael Thorn had ever existed. I could give up the ghost, as Rosie says, and freak out. Or I could be sensible and take care of myself.

So I told myself stories, like those Rosie used to read me, the ones that always had happy endings, no matter how many terrible things happened. I had to keep remembering that. I told myself stories out loud to stop seeing crazy visions. Finally, I guess I fell asleep.

It was superfluous, the next day, when they actually took me to an infirmary. Unlike the white place I had imagined, the infirmary was green.

First, some doctors examined me, listened to my heart, took X rays, made me pee in a cup. They said I was healthy as a horse. I felt hopeful. Maybe I would be sent home.

Then another bunch of doctors began asking questions. Had I ever stuttered, felt like choking, had a lump in my throat? When did I first have trouble speaking and why had I clammed up in juvenile court?

I didn't know how to answer this bombardment. The more they asked, the less I answered.

Part of me wanted to cooperate but another part of me felt scared to death because when I tried to think of helpful replies all I could see in my mind was a long tunnel of nothing.

Finally, a thin man in a brown jacket said I had had enough for one day. He smelled of some kind of sweet tobacco and he put his hand on my shoulder for a brief second.

The idea of happy endings popped back into my mind. It was going to be all right. They would see it was all a mistake. Soon I would be going home. This is when the smirking voice first tried to get into my head. *Happy endings are for assholes*, it said to me, and I was shocked.

An attendant named Harry took me to the green room that I was going to share with a roommate named Freegull. There was nothing about

Freegull that you could like. Everything about him you could hate.

Every morning the first thing I had to look at was Freegull's ugly face, his pockmarked nose and oily skin. He would be there, shouting, "Get up, you piece of shit, get up, you dummy," and yanking the sheets off my bed.

Freegull pulled the sheets on his own bed taut and smacked his pillow into regulation shape. His ambition was to be a trusty, so he could bully the whole school instead of wasting his talents on me. Like the doctors, Freegull wanted answers. He wanted to hear he was the best, pulling me into his face by my tie, asking, "Am I the greatest or what, huh? Huh?"

I had to spend all my energy holding myself together in the green room. I had no time to think of answers, no less give them. I felt like that boy in one of Rosie's stories, holding his finger in the dyke. I couldn't let one crack open in me or I'd explode.

It was easier to just stop talking. But Freegull didn't like having a roommate who couldn't talk. It made him mad, and he would try to force me to yell at him by grabbing me in one of his wrestling locks, squeezing my head or balls, or pressing my eyes until they were ready to pop. I never uttered a sound. It became a matter of wills.

When you're living the Perfectly Normal Life, you cringe at the thought of things like Freegull. If you see a movie about a prison camp, you say to yourself that you couldn't survive. But when you're in the camp yourself, strange things happen.

I forgot the Perfectly Normal Life ever existed. I forgot there was a place where there were things like Lindsay and my buddy Wakefield who had promised me he would organize a coup to get me out of wherever they sent me. Wakefield seemed a million light years away, a pathetically dopey kid who didn't know what life was all about.

I gauged my reaction to life by life at the school. If I got an extra piece of meat in my stew at dinner, it was a good day. If I managed to get to bed without one of Freegull's beatings, it was terrific. If I had the flu and could stay in the infirmary for a week, it was total joy.

In this atmosphere the smallest things become intrigues. And so after a while I created my own intrigue. A secret. One day, when I should have gone back to my room after a totally silent therapy session with Dr. Kline, the thin man in the brown jacket who was now my psychiatrist, I loitered outside his door.

I heard him say, "The boy is becoming a catatonic vegetable," and "God, I just wish I could break through." He was probably talking to another doctor on the phone, but I preferred to imagine him kneeling by the side of his desk, his hands clasped in prayer, which is the typical kind of crazy idea you can get in a place like the school. So I decided Dr. Kline should have his prayers answered, and the next session I began to talk to him. I made him promise not to expect me to talk anywhere else except in his office during our sessions. Soon, he increased the time we met each week from one hour to three.

Dr. Kline was good at theories. One of them was that I was suffering because of my fatherless childhood, that not knowing who my father was had caused all my problems. "This lack of father . . ." he would say, starting out on his theory, and I began to think of it as a disease called *lackafatha*. I didn't want to hurt Kline's feelings, so I didn't tell him that I thought most of his theories were a crock.

One day our comfortable gab sessions ended. Dr. Kline was gone and another doctor, named Painter, took his place. When I asked what happened to Kline, writing the question out on paper, Painter got a funny look and didn't answer. Later, Freegull, gloating because he thought I was stretched out in grief over losing my doctor, told me Kline had been fired.

"Unprofessional behavior," he said with a leer, and made *tsk tsk* sounds, spitting them into my face.

When Rosie came to visit, I told her about the switch.

"It's like nuns," she explained. "In a convent the nuns are not allowed to have a special friend. The school didn't want a doctor having a favorite patient."

It made sense to me. I could understand about favorites. At the school a favorite anything was forbidden. If they found out you liked chocolate pudding, you could bet you would never see a single spoonful while you were there.

Dr. Painter wasn't interested in theories like lackafatha and childhood traumas. He was a health nut and prescribed megadoses of vitamins to cure me.

One day, as I watched him doing his daily jog around the quad, I got a great feeling of weariness. I could see myself spending the rest of my life swallowing pills and staring into Painter's healthy face. I was sick and tired of the school and not talking had become a boring game. I wanted to go back to the Perfectly Normal Life.

So when Painter came in, huffing and puffing, I opened my mouth and talked to him. He was ecstatic. And, after some time, he said he was putting in a recommendation report. I smirked secretly at my cleverness.

But the joke ended up being on me. Getting out of the school had nothing to do with talking. I was due to go when I reached eighteen, and it just happened that I got there at the same time I decided to get cured.

3

So it is a cured me who sits in the kitchen that afternoon, while Rosie is busy with the coffeepot and my grandfather keeps straightening the salt and pepper shakers on the tablecloth, avoiding my eye.

And I think: They don't know what to say to me; now it's them who have mental laryngitis. I imagine the thoughts hurtling around in their heads, rejecting talk about anything that might give us an intimate pain in the heart, looking for clichés, small talk, anything safe, but what is it?

Yet the bland homeliness of the kitchen has a soothing effect and I find myself merging with the shining crystals of the salt, the creamy shape of my grandfather's coffee cup. Rosie pours coffee into it; steaming black stuff that makes me feel good in spite of it all. She raises her own cup like a toast.

"You must be tired," Grandfather says to me. Rosie stands up, wipes her hands down the front of her good black dress like it was some old apron.

Outside, the sky is still blue with deepening evening. The wind swishes through the tree near the back door. Far away, the sound of a dog barking. A long lonesome horn from Monrovia Boulevard takes away the last glint of gold on the shiny windowpanes.

Grandpop suggests I am tired so he can suggest I go to bed. If I'm in bed, I'm out of the way for a while and it's the day over with at last, it doesn't matter that it's early evening and I haven't gone to bed at six o'clock since I was a baby. But I can understand it. Maybe tomorrow, after spending the night together in the house, we can wake up and feel like we belong again.

"Remember the Fryers' cat that used to come over here to visit," Rosie says, "and climb the screen door?" She pauses so that I can remember, and I know I better answer quickly or it will look like I've forgotten, a possibly bad sign.

"Yeah," I tell her, and her face softens with relief.

"Well, he got stuck last week. He was swinging there, flapping every time we opened the door."

Grandpop chuckles.

"Screaming like a banshee," Rosie says. "Scared me to death, his black face looking in at me, spitting and showing his teeth. I thought it was a bat."

"I had to cut him off," Grandpop says, and makes a swipe with his hand. A vision of the poor cat, paws severed, appears in my mind. I see it falling to the porch and limping away on bloody stumps; and the two little cat paws stuck in the screen, bleeding down long rivulets of blood.

"Took out a good piece of screen," Grandpop

says, getting up to show me where he's made a patch. "Silly cat ran off, still hanging on, leaping like a gazelle. Mrs. Fryer had to clip his nails."

I get up to admire the work, wondering if he has a motive. My grandfather is not a handy man. He stays upstairs in his study, writing his papers and letters, unmindful of what needs to be done. "You let the house fall down around your ears," Rosie used to scold. And I was the one who shored things up, who did all the handyman jobs. But in my absence Grandpop seems to have taken over. Does he want my approval? Or maybe he wants to show me I am not indispensable.

"It's a good job," I tell him in a flat voice. His face betrays nothing. His blue eyes look tired.

Up in my room I take off my tie and wonder whether to get into bed. Rosie stands at the door. "Do you need anything?"

A melancholy syrup flows into my throat. "No." My voice is hoarse. "No, thank you."

Rosie peers in at me anxiously. "I put a new box of tissues in the night-table drawer. And there's aspirin and Tylenol in the medicine cabinet."

"Rosie, I'm not sick."

She sets her lips primly. "You're convalescing, it's nothing to be ashamed of. There's no shame in taking time to get your bearings."

She steps into the room an inch, as if she's unused to intimacy with me. Rosie, who came up to kiss me good night until I was fourteen. She makes a gesture with her hand, nodding into the hall. "Don't mind Pop, he's just upset. It's been a long day for him. Go easy tonight." She points to my old black-and-white TV in the corner. The broken antenna is still fixed with black electrical tape. "Keep the TV low," she says. "Relax. There's cold chicken in the fridge. Go down later when he's asleep. I bought you a six-pack of Coke."

"Thanks." I have an overwhelming urge to kiss her cheek, but I squelch it. Rosie looks as awkward as I feel. She hesitates, as if she's making up her mind, then comes forward and gives me a quick peck near my nose. "Sleep tight," she whispers, and runs away.

I shut the door. It has a keyhole, old and painted over, but no key. I used to stick a chair in front of the door to keep them out. Childish. What did I have to hide?

I open my suitcase and start to unpack. I put my travel alarm clock on the windowsill. Rosie sent it to me at school, but I never used it there. You didn't need a clock to know what time it was, they had bells for everything. I kept the clock rolled up in a pair of sweat socks, stuffed in the bottom of my locker, so it wouldn't get ripped off.

I don't have much in the way of clothes. A couple of pairs of jeans, a few shirts, a pullover with a hole under the arm. Six pairs of socks and one extra. Dirty running shoes. My underwear is yellow-gray from the school laundry.

I put everything away neatly, taking time, using time. In the bureau my old clothes are clean and

folded, whiter than white, looking snobbish next to
my dilapidated school remnants.

In the closet more clothes hang, evenly spaced,
my Sunday suit, the blue wool slacks Rosie bought
on sale and I wouldn't wear because they were bell-
bottoms. There's no dust anywhere. It smells of
cedar and bug spray and Rosie's lavender soap.

My desk is polished and the drawers are full of
old school papers and notebooks that Rosie saved. I
put the new school papers on top of them, the ones
telling me how I'm supposed to check in with a
caseworker in Melford, so I can get guidance, so
they can follow up on me. For a moment I wonder if
I am ever going to be through with it. I push the
drawer shut with a bang. If there's one thing I don't
want to do, it's start talking to another psychiatrist.

My room is familiar, yet it feels as if it belongs
to somebody else. That boy Michael Thorn from
then, before everything happened. He *was* somebody
else. I stroll around looking at his possessions, picking them up and putting them down, leafing
through his books, wondering if I liked him or not.

Every once in a while a flutter goes through my
stomach, a tickle of excitement that says: You're
home, you're out, you're really out. *Watch out*, the
smirker in me says, *don't get too high on good because
something bad could happen.*

Faintly, I hear Rosie's voice, telling Grandpop
about the hot-water tap in the bathroom. His voice
rumbles in reply, then their bedroom door is shut.

I feel sorry for my grandfather then. Sorry I

didn't pay more attention to his patch in the kitchen door. I should have admired it more, agreed that it was a good job. I see him standing there, looking so eager, and I get all filled up with regret. It was a way to build a bridge back, and I blew it.

The room is growing dark, shadows of trees dapple the walls. I feel sleepy. Get on the bed and snap on the dim bedside light. Pick up a paperback, *Thus Spake Zarathustra*—God, when did I read that? —and flip through the pages. Words don't make much sense: "Lo, I teach you the superman"—it must have appealed to me for one reason or another. I vaguely remember Wakefield's living room, watching *2001* on his TV. Zarathustra was the strange music associated with the monolith. Well, the book was nothing like the movie, ha ha.

Suddenly I have to sit up and feel my chest. Getting the can't-breathe feeling. Don't panic. I think: Dr. Painter. He'd give me a tranquilizer. There's aspirin and Tylenol in the bathroom cabinet. The idea of walking all the way to the bathroom is overwhelming. A hundred miles, I can't do it.

I'm not going to get scared. It's stupid. But there are no doctors here. It's a funny thing, but I never thought of it. They let me out and now there are no more doctors. They sent me home without a doctor. What am I going to do, living here without a doctor?

"Let yourself flow with it," Dr. Kline used to say. "Don't fight the truth if it wants to reach you."

So what's the big truth that wants to reach me now, here in my own bedroom?

Flow, flow, breathe steadily. You can breathe, it's automatic. Your body takes care of breathing all by itself. You only think you're in charge of breathing but you have nothing to do with it at all.

Dark shadows loom around me and wind rushes past my face. I'm trying to flow with it, but I don't think I like this particular moment of truth. I'm high up, standing at the top of the wall, looking down. Something's crumpled at the bottom. I saw it fall, arcing like a bad dream that can't change its mind; a nightbird flailing its wings as it soared downward. Did I hear the thud or just imagine it?

A screen door bangs shut in my mind. The light comes back. The shadows retreat, the wind stops blowing. I'm sitting on my bed holding a copy of Nietzsche and I'm breathing, I'm still alive. But the taste of the memory is sour.

4

When I was in sixth grade, in the days when they called me Mouse, we had a field day at Monrovia Park. Everyone was told to wear casual clothes and bring a picnic lunch. It seemed very strange to go to school that morning wearing blue jeans. I'd had to show Rosie an official notice so that I could wear them. Until I was ten years old, she dressed me in short pants and Eton jackets. Even in high school Rosie kept trying to get me to wear a tie. One of the things Rosie liked about the special school was that we had to wear ties. It made her feel it couldn't be such a bad place.

But that day in sixth grade we met at the Jefferson Elementary and climbed on a bus to take us to the park. It was a special occasion and everyone was in a frisky mood, wanting to pair off with a friend. But the teachers, insufferable egalitarians, forced us to draw partners from a hat. And I got Ginger McKee.

She held a basket in her lap, sandwiches wrapped in foil, a Snoopy Thermos, and her blue-jeaned leg pressed against mine, especially around the turns. She smelled flowery and kept popping peppermint Life Savers into her mouth. She looked out the window and didn't talk to me.

It was the closest I'd ever been to Ginger McKee, and I sneaked glances at her profile, trying to make up my mind whether or not she was beautiful. Her pink skin was mottled with freckles and I wasn't sure.

By the time we got to the park, I was in love with Ginger. If only she would talk to me, just say one word, it would be the best thing in the world. Nobody talked to me much in that sixth-grade class. They thought I was funny because of my clothes and because I got red in the face and tongue-tied when I had to stand up to give a report.

As soon as we piled out, the enforced partners were forgotten and everybody ran around finding their pals, teasing, joking, yelling.

I wanted Ginger McKee to be my partner in the three-legged race, but she already had her girl friend Mary Ann. I felt miffed. I couldn't think who else might be my partner, nobody wanted me. I skulked around the perimeter of the races, hiding in the dappled shadows under the trees, smelling the grass, feeling full of happiness in spite of myself. After the races and a softball game, in which I was a distant outfielder, it was time for lunch. We all sat down on the grass. Rosie had carefully packed me a proper lunch, chicken-salad sandwiches and raw carrots, but I knew from past experience that the carrots grew limp and the chicken salad warm and smelly, so I'd left the brown paper bag on the bus, under the seat. I only wanted to eat what I had slipped into my pocket that morning: peanuts and a melty Baby Ruth. I sat down on the periphery, between the students and a group of teachers who were drinking coffee, and I ate my peanuts slowly, counting them out. When I bit into the sticky candy bar, I noticed Ginger McKee's eyes watching. Her friend Mary Ann looked, too, and she laughed. But Ginger didn't laugh. She gave me a crooked smile, half-ashamed, and looked back down at her basket of lunch.

It was a sign, I thought, as I gobbled the Baby Ruth. Ginger likes me. Maybe it was the candy, maybe it was my passion for Ginger McKee, but suddenly I was very thirsty. I needed to find a drinking fountain, but I was too shy to ask the teachers.

I must have walked a long way. Although it was only spring, it was hot. The more I walked, the thirstier I got. My tongue felt like fur had grown on it. I wondered how long it took to die of thirst. All sorts of silly ideas crept into my mind on that walk.

Finally, I found a fountain. I took a drink. The water was warm and medicinal, not satisfying at all. I started back, but after only a few steps I was overcome with thirst again. Maybe I did this three or four times, drinking, starting back, returning to the fountain. It became a ritual, something important, like if I didn't go back for *just one more drink*, Rosie would get hit by a car and die, or I would flunk sixth grade or my grandfather would have a heart attack.

Just once more, just once more. After a while I realized I had been away from my class for a long time.

Somehow I got lost then, lost my bearings, and found myself wandering around in unrecognizable parts of the park. I got scared. Suppose they had all climbed back on the bus and left me here? I felt panicky, that it was too late to get back to the bus, too late for everything, that I would never get back home again, even though I knew my way from Monrovia Park blindfolded. I started feeling sorry for Rosie when I thought of never getting home. I felt sorry for the chicken salad sandwiches abandoned under the seat in the bus. This made me feel even sorrier for myself.

When I stumbled onto the class, there were lights flashing all around, from a fire engine and three police cars. The police-car radios were blaring and barking. I felt appalled. What was I going to tell them? That I got lost on the way to the drinking fountain? Yet I also felt pleased that they would care enough about me to call the police and fire department. Still, I felt obligated to give them a reason for all the hullaballoo and I thought I'd better run away and get lost again. But someone spied me and I had to come forward. I decided to limp. I would tell them I had sprained my ankle.

But it wasn't me they were looking for after all. It turned out that one of the students had had an accident. A bunch of them had been grab-assing along the top of the wall of the Greek-style theater. Stone steps climbed up in a semicircle, so people could sit outdoors for the summer concerts. The back of the steps was a sheer drop. A bunch of them had been daring each other to do a tightrope walk on the ledge and someone had fallen off, all the way, six stories down.

There were kids sobbing and mewling, girls mopping their faces, boys looking haunty-eyed. Our teacher, Mrs. Glass, was crying, and two policemen had to hold her up.

"It's my fault," she kept saying, and the policemen tried to shush her.

"Who was it?" I asked someone.

They told me. Ginger McKee.

A long siren came wailing into the park and an ambulance took her away. The teachers herded us back to the bus.

"Is she dead?" everybody wanted to know. "Broke every bone in her body," they speculated. I felt the bus moving, the moving shook me, but I couldn't quite take it all in. I didn't want to bawl or yell. I just sat there, alone on the seat, sliding and slipping around because nobody was next to me.

It wasn't until I got home and remembered that I'd left Rosie's lunch under the seat that I felt a pain. I started crying then. Rosie thought I was crazy, crying over my lost lunch. "What a lot of nonsense," she said.

I kept thinking of that poor sandwich, all by itself somewhere, and it seemed the saddest thing I had ever imagined.

Ginger died. I didn't get to go to her funeral. I

heard about it from Mary Ann, who got friendly with me after that. She said they had tried but they couldn't repair so many broken bones. And I wondered if the bones had stayed inside Ginger's pink, freckled flesh, smashed to smithereens, or whether they had poked through like tree limbs, making her look like ice cracking in the frozen puddles on a winter's day. That's what the other girl's bones looked like. When I found her that night in the park. After the man pushed her. The man they tried to say was me.

5

Sometime during the night, during the fits and starts of my sleeping, I made a decision. I was not going to convalesce, safely tucked away in my bedroom, where I wouldn't cause anybody any trouble with their emotions. I was going out into the world of Kornkill and show my face. I knew what Rosie meant. "Take it easy" was just another way to say "prison."

When the luminous dial of my travel alarm said four o'clock, I decided also that I had to see Lindsay. It came on me like a hot flame, making me jump up and run to the window to see if anybody was awake. Outside, Carhart Street was white with moonlight. The thought of Lindsay was like a pain. How could I have stayed mad at her so long? How come I hadn't rushed to the phone last night?

Wait until morning, I told myself, crawling back into bed to rub my freezing feet against the sheets.

Tomorrow, I promised myself, as I tried to get back to sleep, tomorrow I am going to see Lindsay without fail.

But when morning came, I didn't feel so positive. I felt a little scared about going to Lindsay's house and knocking on her door. I wanted to see her, but I found myself doing it in a roundabout way.

"Where are you going?" Rosie asked, taken by surprise when I came into the kitchen in my sweats. She was still in her pajamas and robe, her hair tied up in a pink scarf, her cheeks all shiny and as pink as the scarf. She had just put on the coffee and was doing her stretches in front of the window: arms up, stretch, to the sides, stretch, down to her knees, stretch, that's as far as she could go. "Where are you rushing to?" she asked. "You have to have your breakfast first." And her voice sounded so forlorn, I came back and sat down, remembering last night and Grandpop and the screen door, not wanting to hurt Rosie's feelings, too.

But I left before Grandpop came down. "I'm going for a run," I told Rosie, and headed up to the cemetery, where Lindsay's Aunt Heva lived. I took the shortcut, through the woods, like we always did when we went to Aunt Heva's.

When we were kids, we used to be afraid to stay after dark. You could see the tombstones from Aunt Heva's dining-room windows. That made supper scary enough, but seeing Uncle Linny come up from the cellar was even scarier. Aunt Heva's husband, Linny Pollard, ran his undertaking business down there. We used to imagine him stirring up big pots of boiling bones. Sometimes, Aunt Heva would say, "Pop down to the cellar and get me a jar of preserves." Lindsay and I went together, shaking and quaking. We never did get to see any bodies, because the undertaking business went on behind a big metal door.

"Can you smell the dead?" Lindsay would ask, and we would stand outside the door and sniff. But it only smelled like a cellar—cool and a little damp.

The shortcut looked the same, just more overgrown. Nobody much used it, except Lindsay and me. Nobody except us ever went to the graveyard so often. It had started out as a lark, Lindsay daring me to come to visit her uncle, the undertaker. But when I met Aunt Heva, I was bewitched. I had never met a character like her before. Lindsay was surprised, maybe even disappointed, that I wasn't scared. Aunt Heva was old and weird and lots of kids were scared of her. But I was used to older people, growing up with Grandpop and Rosie. Aunt Heva and I had a lot in common, since a lot of kids thought I was weird, too.

When I came out of the woods, I saw Aunt Heva sitting on her chair on the porch, even though it was almost October. She was rocking and sewing, a blanket around her knees, her crooked dusty slippers peeking out from underneath.

She jumped when she saw me. She dropped her sewing and put a hand to her throat and said, "Uuuhhh." Then she peered down her nose and let out her breath. "He's not a ghost, he's flesh and blood, thank the Lord for that."

"How could I be a ghost," I asked her, "when I was never dead?"

"I thought you couldn't talk anymore, that's what I heard." She patted the porch with her foot. "Come on, sit down."

"I'm all right," I said. "I'm home for good." But as soon as I said that, I felt my throat go tight. I still had this fear, expecting them to come back, to knock at the door and tell me it was all a mistake. This morning when I woke up, I had been afraid to open my eyes. Afraid that when I did, I'd see Freegull's oily face glowering over me.

Instead, of course, there were Rosie's starched curtains billowing out into my bedroom, the cold autumn air shining in.

Aunt Heva looked me over. It felt good to sit there, absorbing the sun, feeling ordinary.

"You never should have been sent away," Aunt Heva said. She shook her head. "That's the way it is today, the wrong people getting caught. I see in the paper every day that another criminal has been set free without paying for his crime. They get off on a technicality. You should have had a technicality, Michael. It's your grandfather's fault he wouldn't pay for a better lawyer."

I must have made some inadvertent gesture, because Aunt Heva stopped. "No, you don't want to hear it all again," she said. "Tell me, have you seen Lindsay yet?" She cut right to the point, knowing why I was there. Before I could answer, she did herself: "No, you haven't." Her shrewd black eyes glittered in the sun.

"I felt a little funny about it," I said.

She nodded.

"I thought maybe things had changed."

"Things are always changing," she said. "But you don't have to look so grim."

I felt my heart turn over and a little anger start to crackle inside of me. Lindsay had never written to me, in all the time I was at the school. Only sent me cards and signed them "Best, Lindsay," but never sent me a word to let me know what was going on. I used to look for hidden messages in those cards, but all I saw was Santa Claus staring back at me, or some rabbit sitting on an Easter egg. On my birthday she sent one with a lot of balloons coming out of a hat. I figured it was my brains, flying out of my head. I got depressed, but Dr. Kline said balloons were full of hot air and if I had to look for symbols in a birthday card, I should think of the hot air leaving so that cold-blooded reason could come in. Freegull said the balloons were tits. "There's a million tits out there," he said, "that's what it means. You're in here and you can't catch ahold of any of them."

I'd been angry with Lindsay for ignoring me. I still was.

"Do you think it would be all right for me to go over to her house now?" I asked Aunt Heva.

"She's at school now," Aunt Heva said. "You haven't forgotten?"

Of course I hadn't forgotten. It was Monday morning and Lindsay would be in school. She'd be a junior now, maybe had trig with Dr. Flood, the same as I did on Monday mornings.

School. On Mondays we did the laundry at the school. Mondays was steam coming up out of the bottomless laundry sinks and the smell of sweat and soap.

"Of course I haven't forgotten," I said to Aunt Heva, letting a little annoyance show. I had to take a little time, to adjust to thinking the Kornkill way, that's all. This morning, when Rosie asked if I wanted bacon or sausage, I couldn't think of a reply. For two years I'd never had a choice between bacon or sausage. It took time to get into the frame of mind to know if you wanted one or the other.

"Michael? Did I say something wrong?"

I shrugged. It didn't matter.

"I'm sure Lindsay wants to see you. But don't get ideas about going down to the school to wait for her. That wouldn't be an advisable thing to do."

Aunt Heva didn't mind getting to the point. Showing up at the high school might cause a scene. Dangerous Michael Thorn is lurking at the gates!

"I'll wait by the tree," I said. "If she still comes home that way." It was our tree, our waiting place.

Aunt Heva looked twitchy. "Maybe you better wait at home. I'll tell Lindsay. I'll give her a call."

"What's the matter?" I asked. "Does she have a new boyfriend or something? I'm not supposed to know?"

Aunt Heva's neck turned red.

"You can tell me, you don't have to pretend. I'm not going to throw a fit or anything."

Aunt Heva stared at me. "It's up to Lindsay to

tell you about such things, if indeed they need telling. Don't be putting me on the spot, Michael."

I didn't really feel mad at Aunt Heva. It wasn't her fault. But I wished she could lie a little and tell me Lindsay had been pining her heart out for my return.

"Listen to me, Michael, I'm going to tell you something that will help you now." She pulled her chair nearer to me; it squeaked against the porch. "Lindsay's momma, Iraleen, has her shortcomings, but she loves her daughter. She isn't going to let anything happen to Lindsay if she can help it. It's a natural thing and has nothing to do with what she knows in her mind. It's a force that guides her heart.

"So you're not to get upset when you find out Iraleen is against you. She doesn't want to be, but she's afraid. It doesn't matter what I say or Rosie says or some doctor says. This is not a rational thing. Only twice in her life Iraleen has told me to shut my mouth, and this is one of them."

Aunt Heva shook her head and looked out over the cemetery. "I told her to be gentle in her heart and believe in the goodness of God, but she says she's only taking precautions."

I felt the anger rising up in me, so strong it took my breath away. I wanted to scream. I felt like hitting Aunt Heva for telling me. All the time I was preparing to come home, I thought I was preparing myself for this. They're not going to welcome you with open arms, I told myself. Be realistic. People are only human. But I thought it would be hard for them to adjust to my being involved in court, for being a delinquent. Now I wondered: Did they actually think I murdered that girl in Monrovia Park? It seemed so useless, that no matter what was the truth, people harped on the bad stuff, like bad baggage you couldn't put down. It didn't matter if the baggage wasn't yours. You were stuck with it.

"I'm glad you're taking it calmly," Aunt Heva said. "It's the sensible thing." I wanted to laugh. But I knew my laugh would sound crazy, it would frighten Aunt Heva.

"What other time?" I blurted out, to get myself thinking about something else.

"What other time what?" Aunt Heva asked.

"That Lindsay's mother told you to shut up."

Aunt Heva chuckled and I was able to let some of my crazy laughter come out.

"When I told her not to marry Lindsay's father," Aunt Heva said. " 'You shut your advice right up,' she told me. Her heart was set to marry him and nobody could talk her out of it. Now all she does is fret about the man. Well, she's a fretting kind of person. That's why you've got to understand. She can't control her heart."

Aunt Heva went on talking, slipping me the news of the town, filling me in on what had happened while I was away. Every once in a while she'd say, "But Lindsay probably wrote you that," and I thought: See, everybody assumed Lindsay would write to me, they expected her to write to me. I was right to expect it and I'm right for being mad. She's going to have to tell me to my face why she didn't write. She's going to have to tell me to my face that she's like everybody else, that she doesn't believe that I had nothing to do with Monrovia Park.

Maybe I thought Aunt Heva would have all the answers and make everything all right. I guess I always thought she was supernatural. You want to know something, go ask Aunt Heva. She knows it all. We used to think Aunt Heva could put a curse on you. She could give you a hundred years' bad luck by giving you the evil eye. But that was for kids. Aunt Heva was just an eccentric old lady sitting on her porch.

"You better get a job," she was saying now. "Settle in and take up life again."

"A job?" I laughed. "Who's going to hire me? Like Iraleen, the whole town is probably taking precautions."

Aunt Heva scowled. "Don't use my words against me," she said.

"I'm sorry, but it's true. If Lindsay's mother is scared of me, other people will feel the same way."

She nodded. "But you have to start somewhere. So you start simple. Build confidence. It will all blow over after a while. Something else will come along and take people's minds off you."

I wished something would come along right now: an earthquake, a big fire at Krackmayer's factory. Aunt Heva took up her sewing and pushed the needle back and forth in the cloth.

"You start small," she advised, "do something simple."

What I should do was go away and never come back. Go away where nobody knew me. But I looked at Aunt Heva's needle, pulling the thread through the piece of cloth, and I knew Kornkill was like that. Lindsay, Grandpop, Rosie—they were threads running through me, tying in knots on my life.

And anyway, if I went away, I would always wonder about the man in the park. It would always be unfinished.

Dr. Kline's theory was that I had invented the man. Maybe I just wanted my father to be the bad guy, to punish him for not being around all my life. "That's a crock," I told Kline, "because the man was really there." Sometimes, Kline acted like he thought I was guilty, no matter what I told him.

It was better to stay in Kornkill and prove it once and for all. But this idea of a simple job was a figment of Aunt Heva's imagination. Even for simple jobs you had to fill out forms, give your social security number, have references. My references were lousy.

"How about a simple job like a gravedigger?" I said as a joke. But Aunt Heva stopped sewing. "I'll ask Linny," she said. "He might take you on."

I could just imagine Rosie's face. "Aunt Heva, you are too much," I said. I walked back through the woods to Carhart Street. It would never work. A job in the cemetery. Catching death from walking on the graves.

When I came into the kitchen, there was a smell of something cooking. A homemade smell that made my mouth water.

"What are you doing standing there with your mouth open?" Rosie said to me. Her voice was shrill and her face was tense.

"What's the matter?" I asked, suddenly afraid, wondering if they had come knocking on the door, wanting to take me back.

Rosie started to speak, then stopped. She yanked out a chair from under the table and sat down.

"I was going to say it had nothing to do with you," she said in a trembly voice. "But that's not true. It has everything to do with you."

"What is it?" I could feel the panic in my throat. There had been a mistake, I knew it. A mix-up in the release papers . . . something terrible.

"Oh, sit down, you're white as a sheet," Rosie said. She grabbed my hand. "I've got a man coming," she explained. "And I've got to tell him he can't have the room. Pop thinks it's some sensationalizer, coming to gawk at you. But even if he's not, I can't have him here."

I felt relief like hot oil running through my veins. Suddenly my knees were weak and I sat down. "I'm not that famous," I said, trying to cover up how stupid I felt.

But Rosie looked grim. "You don't understand," she said. "I can't let him live here."

"Why not?" Rosie counted on letting the spare

room, it helped with the expenses. Rosie would have turned the whole house into a hotel, but Grandpop, as much as he liked to save money, didn't want an invasion of his privacy. He agreed to just one roomer. We'd had a music teacher and a nurse and finally Miss Crane, who fell down the stairs one Sunday morning and had to move to a place on the ground floor. Rosie had written to me at the school after Miss Crane left, saying she was redecorating in pink and gray. I hadn't thought about the room until now.

"Why not?" I asked again. Rosie looked at me.

"You don't understand. I can't let the room under the circumstances."

"What circumstances?"

Rosie tried to arrange her face in what I recognized as the kind look. She used the kind look for anything unpleasant.

"You ought to know without asking," she said. "But if you insist on hearing it, then I'll have to tell you. I can't be letting the room when there's a murder suspect in the house."

I felt sick to my stomach. "Oh, Rosie," I heard myself moaning.

"I didn't want to say it. But you insisted. As God is my witness, I'm not going to tell you lies. It's not for myself, you understand, I don't think of you that way." She paused, and then went on in a quiet voice, that I could hardly hear. "It's just that I'd never forgive myself if something happened."

"Rosie," I pleaded, ashamed of my weepy voice. "I didn't murder anyone."

"Yes, but we don't know that do we?" she whispered. "We don't really honestly know that for a fact."

6

In the movies, when someone tells the hero something horrible, there's a big crescendo and a fadeout. It's a turning point, a significant moment you can't miss. After that the hero is never the same. He either gets revenge or goes out into the world to do things to prove everyone is wrong about him and gets them to change their minds. Which, when you think of it, is the best form of revenge.

So after Rosie told me she was worried I was going to murder somebody, I figured: This is it. I had the big choice. Revenge would be to pack up and leave.

Do it, kid, the voice in my head said, *they're all a bunch of creeps.*

I went to the bathroom and took two aspirin. Then I took another one, just in case. My head was pounding. I went back to my room and sat on the edge of the bed and thought about going out into the world to prove I wasn't a murderer. That was funny. Having to prove you weren't what you weren't in the first place.

Nobody ever sent me up for murder. Rosie was forgetting that I hadn't gone to the school because I was sentenced for murder. "Your crime is confusion," Dr. Kline used to say. I wished he was here now, or even Painter, I could use a pill or a shot.

In real life, when someone tells you something horrible, you feel mad, carry on, make a fuss, curse them out, but the next thing you know, life is going on and it blows over.

After Rosie said what she did, I banged out of the kitchen, making sure the door slammed hard. Grandpop called downstairs from his room, "What's going on?" and I shouted up, "Nothing!" Then, all was quiet.

For a while I rehearsed the eloquent kind of speech that changes the course of events in a movie. Then I took a nap. When I woke up, it was after lunchtime and I felt hungry. So I went downstairs again. I realized that I had made up my mind. I was going to prove there had been a man in the park. I was going to find him. And he was going to get punished for it and I was going to be in the Kornkill *Journal:* Local Man Is Innocent. The voice in my head said *Sure, Kid.*

Rosie was still in the kitchen. She's always there, and Grandpop is always in his room upstairs. I never remembered anything different. She asked me if I wanted a tuna-fish sandwich. I said yes.

We skirted around each other for a moment, making comments on the weather and discussing whether tuna fish tasted better on white or rye. After a couple of companionable bites, I told Rosie what

Aunt Heva said about Iraleen. Rosie snorted and threw her sandwich down.

"That woman has no common sense," she said. "The worse thing to do is forbid Lindsay to see you. Everyone knows if you tell a child not to do something, he's going to make sure he does it. You have to know about reverse psychology."

"Thanks a lot," I said. Iraleen would tell Lindsay to rush over to see me and Lindsay would refuse. And that's probably what would happen anyway, so maybe this time reverse psychology would help.

"Well, why don't you just call her up?" Rosie said.

I looked up at the kitchen clock. It was a little before three. Lindsay would be home from school. She might answer the phone. Even if she didn't, who would know it was me?

"What's the matter?" Rosie asked.

"I was just thinking. Maybe I shouldn't call. Maybe she doesn't want to talk to me."

Of course she didn't want to talk to me. What was I, crazy? She didn't write to me for two years. You can't count Christmas cards, you send those to anybody. She didn't write and she wasn't flying over here herself, she wasn't letting me know she was waiting with open arms. I was crazy.

"Nope," I said, stuffing the last of the tuna fish into my mouth. "I'm not gonna do it."

Rosie looked annoyed. "She's your friend, Mickey. She wrote to you almost every day. You can't hold what her mother thinks against her."

I was trying to swallow the tuna fish, so all I could do was grunt. Rosie was rambling on. "It's like *Romeo and Juliet*. Why should young people suffer because the adults disagree?"

I swallowed. "Rosie, I don't think *Romeo and Juliet* exactly applies here. And anyway, I never got a single letter from Lindsay."

And anyway, I felt like telling her, why should prospective boarders suffer because adults think I'm a murderer? But I didn't say anything. Rosie's the kind of person who can have two opposite opinions in her head at the same time. Grandpop says it's because of her religion.

Rosie's eyes popped open when I told her about the letters. "The bastards!" she shouted. "Excuse me. They must have absconded them."

"Who?" I asked her. "Somebody took them?" It was beginning to sound like a movie again.

"The school authorities," Rosie explained. "Not absconded, I mean impounded. Whatever they do when they won't let you read a letter in a prison."

For a moment I felt a twinge of hope. But Rosie was wrong. I had got all of Rosie's letters that complained about the conditions on her last visit, like urine stains in the back courtyard and dustballs on the stairwells and no tissue in the ladies' room. What could Lindsay have written that would be censored?

It was just a case of assumption. Rosie and Aunt Heva, Our Ladies of Assumption. Nobody could believe Lindsay wouldn't write to me. Everybody believed I was innocent, in public. In private it was another story. I bet if Rosie met Iraleen on the street, Iraleen would say, "Why hasn't Mickey called Lindsay yet?" In private she was taking precautions, feeling scared. When one of the kids in ninth grade was in the hospital with leukemia, we all signed a giant-sized card and sent it to him. "Get well soon, Bobby." The student council organized it. They didn't organize any card for me. I'd never heard from them.

"You're looking down in the dumps, worse than ever," Rosie said.

"Everybody is afraid of me!" I shouted at her. "Lindsay didn't write because she's like all the rest of the frightened sheep."

"I don't know what you're talking about," Rosie said. "And while I'm reminded, that friend of yours phoned up this morning. I had so much on my mind, I forgot to tell you."

"What friend of mine?" I laughed scornfully. Rosie shook her head and got up to search for her glasses and a scrap of paper. "That heavyset boy," she said, rummaging in a pile of coupons. "He had a name like a dog."

"God, you don't mean Wakefield?"

Rosie thrust the scrap of paper at me. It said, simply, "Wakefield," and there was a phone number. It was the name "Laddie" that Rosie remembered, although he hadn't been called Laddie Wakefield in years.

"So, what about the frightened sheep now?" Rosie said snappishly.

"Wakefield was always a friend," I said. But it's true, I had lumped him in with the sheep.

"And did he write to you every day?"

"Who, Wakefield? He wouldn't write. It's not his thing."

"So what are you worried about, then?" Rosie asked. "What difference does it make if Lindsay wrote or not?"

I groaned. Rosie had this habit of twisting everything around so that it came out even. "But you *said* Lindsay wrote, and her Aunt Heva said she wrote, but I never got any letters. It's the pretense that makes me mad."

"People put too much stock into things like letters," Rosie said. "It's what's in the heart that counts. Your grandfather hasn't given me a card or written me a letter in the twenty years we've been married."

"Yeah, well, he didn't write to me, either," I said. I slammed out of the kitchen for the second time that day. Rosie was scolding from behind the door. "Listen to me young man, you can't . . ." just like it was the old days.

From upstairs Grandpop shouted: "What's going on?"

"Nothing!" I shouted back.

I think I've gone from one crazy house to another. Yesterday, it seemed good to be home. Today, it seems like the nuttiest, stupidest, most ridiculously dumb idea I ever had.

7

"Nothing was what was going on before," Grandpop said, peering down the stairs with his reading glasses on the end of his nose. His face was stern. "I can't get any work done if there's an explosion every hour on the hour."

"I'm sorry," I said, and he went back to his room and shut the door. My grandfather is an *ologist*, I used to say. When they asked us in grade school, "What does your father do, what does your mother do," I would answer that my grandfather was my father and he was an ologist. That was because Grandpop was always pursuing some course of study, archaeology, or entomology, or anthropology. He liked bugs best and wrote papers about them and even had his writing published in special magazines for other ologists. My grandfather had two pensions, one from the army and one from the fire department. He retired early and began locking himself in his upstairs study. Sometimes it smelled of formaldehyde and sometimes of mothballs, depending on what he was studying. He had millions of spider parts in tubes with rubber stoppers. And he had boxes of dead butterflies, skewered through the heart, sprinkled with mothballs to keep the other bugs out. I used to think it was the funniest thing, to use mothballs on butterflies. I used to tell things like that to the kids and I got a reputation for being a flake.

When Grandpop went back to his room, I thought about calling Wakefield. The telephone was sitting there in the hall, looking at me, daring me to do it. Call Wakefield, call Lindsay. Wakefield was easier, so I picked up the phone and dialed. Grandpop would raise a stink about long distance before five o'clock, but I didn't care. Pretty soon I was going to make money as a gravedigger.

The area code was 413 and I wondered if Wakefield had gotten his dream of going to Dartmouth. I dialed eleven numbers and waited and I felt scared shitless all of a sudden. Somebody, not Wakefield, answered and I hung up before they could even finish saying hello the second time. What was I going to say to Wakefield? "Hey, buddy, how come you didn't get me out of that place like you promised?" Wakefield was in some flashy college and I was embarking on a career in the graveyard. I wondered how he figured I was home. Maybe his mother had told him.

So when are you going to start on your mission? the smirking voice asked me.

Right now, I told it. Right now, I'm going to go over to see Lindsay. What had I been thinking about? The poor kid was grounded, locked in her room. I'd been thinking of Lindsay not wanting to see me. But this was the Perfectly Normal Life and kids did what their parents told them to. Lindsay was just a high school kid, a baby. She was probably trying to think of a way to sneak out but just hadn't had the opportunity yet. But that's all it was. I had to get my perspective back. Parents and kids, not fortresses and bodyguards. What the heck was I afraid of?

I opened the closet and found my bulky knit sweater still hanging on the hook in the back. My running shoes got all wet earlier so I crawled down in the darkness to scrounge for my old Wellington boots. I felt good now that I had a plan, was doing something positive. Maybe Lindsay could help me find the man who had been in the park that night. It wasn't Lindsay's fault, she was a victim of circumstances, just like me. I'd even forgive her for being a sheep. A sixteen-year-old kid couldn't help it.

But no sooner did I bubble to a boil with all these wonderful plans than I burned myself out. Who was I kidding? Lindsay and me going out to find clues? Solving the Mystery of Monrovia Park. What a joke.

What did I tell you? the voice said in my head. *Don't count your eggs before they hatch. Don't put them all in one basket. An apple a day keeps the doctor away.*

I slammed my fist into the side of the closet to make it stop.

The knocker boomed on the front door. Rosie burst out of the kitchen and rushed past the closet, not even noticing me crouching there like a gnome.

"Mr. Longman," I heard her say in a syrupy voice. "Come in."

She pulled the door open and then she saw me. Her face went pale and she gave a twitch of a jump; I could see she was trying to control herself, but she was scared.

"Michael! Why on earth are you hiding in there?"

"I'm not hiding," I said, trying to stand up and act nonchalant. "I was looking for my boots." I noticed my boots had somehow put themselves into my hands. "Found them," I said, and I could feel my stupid grin slop across my face. From behind Rosie a tall bearded man peered quizzically at me.

The fear still in her eyes, Rosie mumbled an apology and hustled him off into her needlepoint-and-velvet parlor. I dropped the boots and came out of the closet. Rosie shut the parlor door. Feeling sick and excited, I went over, walking very quietly, and listened.

Gary Longman was his name. He made himself sound like a big deal. He was going to do great things in life, I could hear it. It was in his voice, a sort of uncontrollable brag.

Rosie kept making excuses, deprecating the facilities, trying to put Longman off. One thing Rosie was not, she was not a liar. She could have just told him, "Sorry, the room is rented." Instead she made a mess of it. Finally, I heard her say, "Do you know where you are, Mr. Longman?" Her voice was full of doom. But he laughed and said, "Of course I know where I am," and there was an undertone of annoyance in his words.

"Well, then, you understand why I can't let you have the room," Rosie said. Her voice screeched out, as if she was at her wit's end: "You're in the house of Michael Thorn!" Like an Edgar Allan Poe announcement. There was a big silence. I expected Gary Longman to scream back: "Oh, no! Not Michael Thorn!"

"Well, I know that," he said in a perfectly normal voice. "That's precisely why I came. I'm planning to write a book."

I could hear Rosie gasp through the door: "Sensationalizer!"

Longman protested. "I don't want to sensationalize anything. I abhor that sort of thing. I'm planning to do a serious study."

"It was already in the newspapers," Rosie said. "There's nothing left to write about."

"I'm looking for the story behind the story," Longman said, and his voice had the brag in it again. "The truth. What if Michael is innocent? No, what am I saying, Michael *is* innocent, right? I want to show how the truth can get distorted, how the most ordinary series of events can turn the tide. . . . I want to—"

Rosie interrupted. "This is a real book you're writing? It's going to have your name on the cover?"

"Look, you can check my references. I'll give you the names of some people. My boss is the editor of the Canuga *Post*. He'll vouch for me."

"A reporter," Rosie snorted accusingly.

"I'm a serious journalist," Longman said, sounding hurt. "And I'm here in search of the truth."

I could hardly keep myself from bursting into the room. My heart was thumping like I was having a heart attack. But if Rosie knew I had been eavesdropping . . . I heard Grandpop come out of his room. He was coming to the stairs.

"It's past dinner," he was grumbling. Then he spied me. "Michael, what are you doing there in the dark? Put some g.d. lights on in this house."

I snapped the hall switch and jumped back into the closet, because Rosie was coming out of the sitting room. "It's nothing fancy, you understand. . . ." she was saying to Gary Longman.

I heard Grandpop's exasperated, "What now?" and his footsteps running back to his study so he wouldn't have to meet Rosie's boarder. I chuckled inside the closet, thinking of the two of us, hiding from Rosie, and wondered what Gary Longman would think if he knew.

At the dinner table Rosie said, "I've rented the room." She looked across at me with a stare that dared me to open my mouth about her previous doubts. I just looked back.

"To who?" Grandpop asked.

"A writer. He's writing a book."

Grandpop looked up from his plate and Rosie rushed on, "It's a bona fide book. He has what they call an advance. And good references. I'll be checking up on him before he moves in."

"What about his habits?" Grandpop asked. "Writers smoke and drink."

"He doesn't smoke," Rosie said. "I would never let a smoker into the house." She knew Grandpop sneaked a cigar in his study. He was only supposed to smoke out on the porch. She passed me the potatoes. She passed Grandpop the meat.

"What kind of book?" Grandpop asked. "Probably a thriller. That's all people read now, they want thrills. When I was a boy I read the classics. I don't suppose he's writing a classic."

I laughed and Grandpop smiled at me.

"Oh, who knows, it may well be something good," Rosie said in a sly way. I pretended not to notice and went on eating my potatoes. But inside I was shouting and jumping around and feeling glad. I couldn't wait for Rosie to tell us about Gary Longman's book. A book to prove I hadn't been imagining things that night in Monrovia Park. Tell, Rosie, tell.

But Rosie started to talk about whether she should get the gateleg table out of the attic so the boarder could use it for a desk. "There's no real desk in that room," she said, thinking aloud. "He'll need a place to put his typewriter."

I stuffed potatoes into my mouth and clunked my teeth with the heavy silver fork. I wasn't used to such forks. At the school we had small lightweight knives and forks and you had to be sure you turned

them in after you ate or there was a search. I used to
wonder if anybody ever succeeded in stabbing anyone to death with a miserable tin school-fork. The
potatoes tasted like dust. I was too excited to eat. I
wanted Rosie to tell about Longman's book.

"Well, it will bring in the extra money," Rosie
was saying.

"And what about you?" my grandfather asked,
suddenly turning to me. "What about the next
step?"

"The next step?" I asked back stupidly. They
had been talking about money. "Oh, you mean get a
job?"

"That's the general idea. Make a living like everyone else."

"There's plenty of time for that," Rosie said.
"Let him be for now." She handed Grandpop the
platter of meat. "Here, have another slice."

"The boy should get a job," Grandpop said,
pushing the platter away.

"In good time," Rosie said. "He needs a rest.
He needs time to convalesce."

They began to bicker. And Rosie kept making it
seem as if I was an invalid who couldn't work, and
then she hinted that maybe it would be hard for me
to find a job. And then she forgot I was sitting there
and said to Grandpop, "Now you tell me who is
going to hire him?" She shrieked it. "Now you tell
me that!"

They began shouting at each other.

"I have a job," I said.

There was dead silence. They looked at me.

"I'm going to work up at the cemetery."

They kept looking at me like they didn't believe it.

"You know, digging. Digging graves."

Grandpop started to laugh first, then Rosie. "Oh, Mickey, you're such a card," she said, wiping away tears.

"It's true," I said.

"Oh, Michael, you can't work in a graveyard."

"Why not?" I asked her. "It's a fitting position for a murderer."

"Jesus Christ!" Grandpop boomed. He hit the table with his fist.

"Now, don't get excited, Mickey didn't mean it. Michael, see what you've done! Michael how could you?!" Rosie was trying to keep Grandpop from falling out of his chair, from hacking the table with his knife, from coming after me with it. "Michael, come back here!"

But I picked up my plate and brought it to the kitchen and scraped it off and put it into the sinkful of soapy water that Rosie always had ready for after dinner. I could hear their voices in the dining room, Rosie's persistent hum, Grandpop's rumbles.

I felt smug. Call a spade a spade. If you can't take it, don't dish it out.

Watch it, the smirky voice said, but for the first time it sounded uncertain. *If you play with fire, you can get burned.*

Not applicable, I told it back.

"Go tell your grandfather you're sorry," Rosie said, coming into the kitchen with a stack of plates.

"Why should I?"

She gave me a long look. Behind her eyes the truth of what she was about to say was shining, a glimmer of unspent tears, it transcended her.

"Because I was the one who doubted you," she said. "He never did, not for a minute."

When I went back into the dining room, my grandfather was gone. I heard his step rounding the top of the stairs. Moments later his door shut.

I'm scared, I thought. It had seemed like a good idea to play it like in the movies but it wasn't working out too well in real life. These dramatic moments don't fade out, life keeps going on.

I thought of how I had never really had a private conversation with my grandfather. I thought about how I always had this funny feeling that he would tell me something I couldn't stand to know. Like where my father was, or why my mother died, or, worst of all, that he loved me.

8

Now or never, now or never, the words kept flashing in my mind, playing themselves like a drum roll, keeping to the beat of my feet as I moved through the darkness on my way to Lindsay's house.

Now or never is what I'd told myself in the mirror as I brushed my teeth before going to bed. If I didn't get it straight with Lindsay now, I never would.

The whole evening at home had been a disaster. I had gone upstairs and knocked on my grandfather's door. He said, "Come in," and I went in and stood there. And he sat there, behind his table which was covered with notebooks, papers, Petri dishes; rubber-stoppered vials of dead bugs, and gleaming instruments of bug dissection. But before he let me start to talk, he covered his microscope with the gray cloth, as if my talking might get germs on it. Rosie'd told me his microscope had cost more than a thousand dollars but you can't believe everything Rosie says about prices, she gets things out of proportion.

"I'm sorry," I said, and in that moment I had no

idea what I was sorry for, although I felt sadder than I had ever felt.

"It's all right," my grandfather said in a very formal way. "I know you're under a strain. Who wouldn't be in the circumstances?"

The way he said it, as if he really did understand, made me want to stay and talk more, the first time in my life I can remember having such a feeling with my grandfather. But he dismissed me, turning back to his books and bugs.

So I went out again and shut the door and saw Rosie halfway up the stairs, listening.

"You didn't have to check up on me," I said.

"What are you going to do now?" she asked, almost as if she thought I was going to attack her.

I consciously moved back, to give her room, to make her feel safe. "Go to bed, what else?" I said casually. "There's nothing else to do around here."

She sighed. "If you watch TV, keep it low." She went back downstairs and I heard her clanking around in the kitchen. She would probably start cleaning the oven or something. Rosie did things like that when she was upset.

I made all the preparations for going to bed. I took a shower because I realized I stank in the dirty sweats I still had on since the morning, and I washed my hair and brushed my teeth, and it was when I was looking at my face in the mirror that it came to me: Now or never. You either go over to see Lindsay now or you forget it for good.

It's stupid to give yourself ultimatums like that.

But sometimes it's survival. I learned it to survive with Freegull. Once he pushed my head down into the sink in the green room, when the sink was full of water. He had my hands behind me and I couldn't move, and I told myself I was going to pull out the stopper with my teeth because I wasn't going to drown just for Freegull. And I had to get at the chain with my tongue, and hold my breath at the same time and my neck and lungs were killing me and I thought, You are going to get that chain on the next try or you are going to let yourself drown. Freegull was pissed when the water went gurgling down the drain.

After the shower, after neating up the bathroom so Rosie wouldn't get mad and want to come into my bedroom to complain, I went back and got dressed again. I waited until I heard her finish in the kitchen. Around ten o'clock I stuffed my bed up a little with an old blanket and turned off the light and crept out. I went down the hall to one of the spare rooms and let myself out the window onto the top of the kitchen porch roof. Nobody would notice an unlocked window in the spare room, but Rosie was likely to check the front door to be sure the chain was on at least five times a night.

Then I ran down Carhart Street to Lindsay's house.

Running. Always running somewhere to find her, to see her, to catch up with her. She was like a high flying wind, always on the move, her hair streaming out behind her like the tail on a tornado.

A small bird who doesn't know it's an eagle inside. Honey feathers and bluewater eyes. She would stand on a hill and look far away into the distance and say, "Mickey, don't you wish we could go someplace really exciting?"

When I got to her house, I didn't know what to do. I heard a dog set up a fuss somewhere down the street and I froze until it stopped. It was one lucky thing that Lindsay's mother was allergic to animals and they had no dog. Lindsay had always been sad she couldn't have a cat. She would have named it Mouse; that was a joke for me.

Her window was the one on the left side upstairs. It was lighted up. She was in there. It made me mad, looking at that lighted window. Damn you, Lin, how could you just sit up there in your room and not care about me anymore?

Her father's truck was in the driveway on the same side. Somebody was in the living room, watching TV, because I could see the flicker of bluish light. I climbed up on the back of the truck, then up on top of the cab. I could just about get my head level with her windowsill. I whispered: "Lindsay." I willed her to come to the window and look out. But nothing happened.

I climbed down again, got some pebbles from the driveway, and climbed back up. Everybody knows how to do it, you throw stones at your girl friend's window and she sticks her head out and smiles and says, "Hi." I threw the pebbles and one of them made such a crack on the glass I thought it would break. The rest all fell down on top of the truck and clunked and rattled like a meteor shower. Down the street the dog set up a racket again and I thought I heard a man's voice say, "What the hell's that?" Then Lindsay's light went out.

Shit. It was never.

Why don't I just knock on the door like a civilized person? I had a right to do it. Instead, I skulked off into the woods in the back of the house and crouched down there, waiting.

The back-porch light snapped on and Lindsay's mother opened the door and put a black plastic bag into the trash can. I gave her the finger. That's for you, Iraleen.

Something was rustling around in the leaves nearby. I hoped it wasn't the dog. I hoped it wasn't something that was going to bite me. Iraleen was still on the porch, fixing some mops and rags that were hanging on a rack. This thing kept rustling along nearer and nearer, and I didn't dare move.

Ignominious was the word I thought then. That said it all.

This big raccoon trotted right past me, his bandit face staring straight ahead, making for the garbage can. He didn't even care that Iraleen was on the porch. He got there just as she went back inside. He reached up and took the lid off the can just like he was human. I got the feeling I was having a hallucination. I got up and ran back down the side of the house and when I got to the front, I stopped and yelled "Lindsay!" just once, but loud, and then I took off running.

At the corner I stopped and waited. But the street was quiet, not even the dog was barking.

And then, like a slow fudge dream, a police car came nosing around the corner from Monrovia Boulevard, sliding into the street like a sneaky stream of piss. Without flashers, without a siren, it crawled toward Lindsay's house, and I could see the two guys in the front. One of them was Charlie Melville, who had taken me to the station two years ago. His beaky nose was trying to sniff me out. Lindsay's parents had called the cops.

I really ran then, taking a shortcut through the woods and people's backyards. I ran like hell and I was going so fast, I had only a split second to register that somebody was standing right outside my house. I thought: They've got the place surrounded —and then I ran right into him.

But this person I collided with seemed about as scared as I was. He backed off, with his hands up in a sort of supplicating gesture. "Look, take it easy," he said, and then he stopped and looked at me. "Michael Thorn?"

"Gary Longman?"

We shook hands.

"Hey," he said, "you don't know how lucky this is. I knew it was too late to ring the bell, but I thought, wouldn't it be great if the kid came out so we could talk."

His voice had that braggy sound to it and it was loud.

"Ssssh," I said, and he said, "Oh, sorry," and looked at the dark house.

"I guess they're asleep, huh?"

"No, it's not that." I grabbed his arm and pulled him. "We gotta get out of here."

"What's the matter?" he asked, sounding alarmed, but he came along with me and we went behind the house. I wondered if I should take him up to my room with me. I wondered if he could climb up on the porch roof.

"The cops," I said, but I could see from his face he thought I was having a delusion. So I explained about being at Lindsay's.

I was amazed by the change that came over his face. Even in the dark I could see he was angry. He smacked his fist against the palm of his hand. "Now, see, that's just what I'm talking about. Here's an example of just what I've been working on. I can't believe it, it's right here in my lap. I knew it! I knew it when I first got the idea and I told Jake . . ."

I didn't know what he was babbling about, but it felt good that somebody should get angry with the cops and be on my side.

"Excuse me," I said, "but I don't think we can just stand here talking."

"Sorry. Of course. I shouldn't be here anyway. But I couldn't sleep and I thought I'd take a walk and—"

"Excuse me," I said again. "I gotta go." I could

see the gleam of Charlie Melville's banana boat coming down Carhart Street. I got up on the porch rail, hoisted myself to the roof, and was inside the window in a flash. I waited, holding my breath, wondering if Longman had been smart enough to keep out of sight. Nothing happened, and after a while I sneaked out of the spare room and went to the bathroom, where I could look out at the street. It was empty. I flushed the toilet, just in case Rosie had heard me moving around, and went back to my bedroom.

I was all sweaty and I stank again but I got into bed and pulled the covers up. It was a comfortable stink; I knew I was alive.

I fell asleep and dreamed about everything that had just happened. Except in the dream it was Lindsay who was driving the police car and Rosie who was putting out the garbage and instead of a raccoon, a long bumpy revolting alligator came out of the woods and headed for Rosie, mouth open, teeth shining. I tried to warn her but when I opened my mouth, nothing came out.

I didn't want to watch Rosie get chewed up, so I ran. I must have run for hours and I was tired. I stopped to rest by the gates of the cemetery. And suddenly it was bright daylight and the sky above me was gleaming and it opened up like the curtains being pulled apart on a stage and Gary Longman was there, looking like God. I was filled up with a feeling of peace and happiness, so good that I wanted to burst.

It's just a dream, I told myself in the dream, but I wasn't disappointed. I had a feeling that from now on, everything was going to be all right.

9

The telephone rang early in the morning. We were in the kitchen and Rosie got up and went to answer, her slippers slushing across the floor. Grandpop said, "Who's that?" and Rosie threw back over her shoulder, "I'll know when I answer, won't I?"

It was a grouchy morning, clouded over, the sky dead lead. The kind of morning that gives you a headache, but I felt relatively terrific because Gary Longman was moving in this afternoon. And maybe it was Lindsay on the phone. Ha Ha.

My heart kicked over when Rosie came back and said, "It's for you." Her face gave nothing away. I rushed out, knocking my juice glass over. I grabbed the phone, said hello, and heard Aunt Heva's voice.

"I spoke to Linny about the job," she said. "And he thinks you might give it a whirl. He'll teach you how to use the backhoe. Now, isn't that good news?"

I said sure, but I wasn't exactly enthusiastic.

"Why don't you come up here this afternoon?" Aunt Heva went on. "Make it around two thirty. If you wanted to stop by Murworth's Tomb before you

came on in to see Linny, I wouldn't be surprised."
There was gleeful conspiracy in her words.

"I'll come, I'll be there," I said. "I'll be up there
at two thirty."

"All right Michael," Aunt Heva said. "Watch
you don't blow a gasket."

When I came back to the table, Rosie looked at
me hard.

"It was Mrs. Pollard," I said. "About the job." I
felt my face go hot.

"I *know* it was Heva Pollard," Rosie said. She
looked at Grandpop. "And it's all right about your
working up there."

"A job is a job," Grandpop said. "But I hope
you don't want to make a career of it." He caught my
eye. It was all right. I laughed and he smiled. He
wiped his mouth with his napkin. "And speaking of
jobs, I've got one to get to myself, up in my study."

Rosie shook her head. That meant, "Some
job!" When he was gone she said to me, "There's a
lot to do around here, too, you know. I don't know
what hours you're going to be keeping, up there
digging graves. But when you get yourself organized, you tell me if you can spare a little time." She
started clearing the dishes, looking more hurt than
angry.

I remembered how I'd felt when I first came
home and stepped out of the taxi. Only the day
before yesterday; it seemed a hundred years ago.
The porch needed painting, I'd noticed. Things had
a neglected look. And I'd been mad when I thought

Grandpop was taking over my duties as the handy-man.

"Don't worry, Rosie, I'll do everything you want," I said. "I can start right now. I'm not going up to the cemetery till later."

"Well, then, get that table out from the attic for Mr. Longman's room. And maybe you can tidy up the yard."

I did everything Rosie asked. On the third floor was a big storage attic and the boarder's room and bath, completely separate from the rest of the house. I carried the gateleg table into the room and saw that Rosie had decorated it in pink and gray, just like she'd written in her letter. It looked a very wom-anish room and I wondered how Gary Longman was going to like it. He'd probably want the dressing table taken out. It had an organdy skirt and a lot of glass perfume bottles on the mirrored top. I thought I'd tell Rosie to get rid of it. But then I just took the bottles off, picked the thing up, and carried it to the attic. In its place I put the gateleg table. I found a chair, too, so he could really set up his desk. He'd need a good lamp. The room was full of pint-sized lamps with pink shades. He could have mine. Heck, I wasn't going to be studying anymore. I went down and brought it up. And I brought him my matching fake-leather pencil holder and blotter pad that Rosie had given me when I was twelve. I ar-ranged it and stepped back to look it over. Not a real desk like he was probably used to writing on, but not bad.

Then I went out and raked all the leaves in the yard and stuffed them into plastic bags. I started pulling out the dead marigolds that Rosie had grown along the borders. And all the time I was thinking of Murworth's Tomb and felt joy exploding in my stomach.

There were three tombs in the cemetery, all of them very old. Nobody could afford fancy mausoleums these days, Aunt Heva said. They looked like miniature Greek temples to me, little white houses with stone pillars and windows like a church. Linny always made sure the grass was trimmed and the bushes pruned, and in the summer they were spilled over with roses. And the one that had MURWORTH cut in deep sharp letters over the pillars, Lindsay and I had discovered was unlocked.

We'd been afraid to go inside at first. Lindsay said it might be like King Tut's tomb, where if you went in, you got cursed. So we just peered around the door. It was bare and cold, nothing scary about it at all. We kept daring each other but neither of us would cross the threshold. Finally, one time when we were having supper at Aunt Heva's, I asked who Murworth was.

"Before my time," Linny said, and shrugged, but Aunt Heva wanted to know why I asked.

"I was wondering if any of those tombs had curses on them," I told her. You could say something like that to Aunt Heva and she would consider it seriously and give you a straight answer. You could say something like that to Rosie, too, and she would take it just as seriously. But Rosie didn't have the witchy knowledge Aunt Heva had.

"Benign," Aunt Heva proclaimed. "All three of the mausoleums are benign. If you want a curse, you go over to the grove end and look for Mary Owen's tombstone. She's the type for a curse."

"Don't go scaring the kids," Linny protested.

"You know yourself the grass won't grow on that grave," Aunt Heva said. "And a flower will never bloom."

Linny shook his head. "That's because there's no sun on the spot."

Aunt Heva ignored him. "The Murworth family were nice people and rich. They left a fund to build the hospital in Melford."

It was fitting, then, that Lindsay and I first played doctor in Murworth's tomb. We put poultices of leaves and spit on each other's arms and legs and stomachs. Lindsay wouldn't let me look below her belly button, but she let me inspect her chest. We compared chests and nipples and decided hers were ugly. Lindsay said she was worried about growing out into breasts. She said she would never be able to run as fast with breasts.

I didn't let her see past my belly button, either, although I would have, if she had been fair. We played doctor a whole summer, until it got too cold to take off our clothes in Murworth's Tomb. And when it warmed up again, the following year, something had happened that made it impossible to play doctor again. We were shy with each other and one day I saw that Lindsay had grown breasts.

I touched Lindsay's breasts in Murworth's Tomb. We weren't playing doctor, we were standing in the dark, breathing into each other's ears and mouth and making noises I had never heard us make before. It just happened, on the way back from supper at Aunt Heva's. She wouldn't let me get past her belly button, she wouldn't let me put my tongue into her mouth.

In the green room Freegull used to talk about solidified cases of frustration. He would look at pictures in his magazines and yell, "God, it's killing me!" But I never felt frustrated with Lindsay. The warmth of her, the tingling she created in me, it was mysterious, sensuous, it always seemed right. Not that I didn't try. I did. But Lindsay said no. And I went home happy. I went home feeling Lindsay was being sensible. We could wait. I even felt noble about it all.

Aunt Heva always knew we went to Murworth's Tomb and she always looked the other way. It occurred to me now that this was a very quirky thing to do. It wasn't what you'd call regular adult behavior. I stopped raking to think about this, seeing Aunt Heva in a new light, not really understanding why.

Aunt Heva was married to Linny Pollard, who was Iraleen's brother. Lindsay was named after her Uncle Linny. Was it because Aunt Heva wasn't a blood relation that she didn't care if we were making out in somebody's tomb? But Rosie wasn't a blood relation and I couldn't see her looking the other way.

I was thinking about this when I heard a voice from the other side of the fence. It was Mrs. Dullea from next door.

"Congratulations!" she said to me, and stood there, smiling.

"Yeah, thanks," I said. I guess she meant well. I didn't know what else to say to her. Rosie and Grandpop had never been very friendly with the neighbors. Rosie says it's better that way, then you don't have to feel awkward when it comes to complaints. The neighbors on the other side kept changing, but Mr. and Mrs. Dullea had been in their house since I was a kid. She used to give me Hershey's chocolate kisses for trick or treat. She looked the same, all these years, wearing a flowered kind of coverall over slacks, her grayish-brown hair short and curly. She waved at me and went inside her house.

"What did she want?" Rosie asked when I came into the kitchen for a drink.

"She was just saying hello, is that okay with you?"

"Aren't we snappy today?"

"Look, I'm doing the work and I'm minding my own business, okay?"

"And what's that supposed to mean?" Rosie asked as I put the glass on the drainboard and went out again.

That you should mind yours, I thought. I was

still pissed with Rosie for not telling me about Gary's book. But now it was becoming a game of who could hold out longest. Maybe she was just going to let him tell me himself, and maybe that was the right thing to do.

It was getting on toward two o'clock and I was getting antsy. I was sorry to miss Gary's moving in but I wanted to get dressed and see Lindsay.

In my mind I could see her the way she'd been before I went away: fourteen years old, wearing a yellow sweat shirt and jeans, her hair tied in a yellow band. It was the morning I had to appear in juvenile court. I heard her downstairs, talking to Rosie, and Rosie was saying I'd be right down for my breakfast. But I stayed in my room. I couldn't face Lindsay. I felt too embarrassed. "Mickeeeee!" she called up the stairs, "Come on, will you? I gotta go to school." Finally, when I heard the front door slam, I looked out the upstairs window and saw her walking away down Carhart Street, her head bent over her books. Then Rosie's friend Moira drove up and honked and Rosie and Grandpop and me went off to the hearing.

Lindsay wasn't fourteen anymore. And all I could think of was the tomb and the dark and playing doctor so long ago. It made my heart feel funny. I gulped air and worried if I was going to get one of my can't-breathe attacks that would spoil it all. I felt naked without my doctors and my pills. What I needed was a Valium. How could they send me home without any pills? *Because they're assholes,* the smirky voice said in my head and for once I agreed wholeheartedly.

I took a shower. Rosie came upstairs and banged on the door, like she was afraid I was doing something dirty. "What're you in the shower for?" she yelled in at me.

"Close the goddamn door!" I shouted back. She was letting in a freezing draft. I heard the door slam shut and I wondered if she had come into the bathroom. I was almost afraid to look out from behind the curtain. It would be just like Rosie. Never mind privacy, never mind you were no kid anymore. She probably thought she was going to wash behind my ears.

But she wasn't there. She was waiting in the kitchen when I came down. There was a cup of tea cooling next to her and the paperback she was reading was spread-eagle next to it, just the way she told me never to put a book down, because it would ruin the spine.

"I want you to reconsider your language, if you please," she said. I stared hard at the book, hoping she'd see I noticed.

"It was cold with the door open," I said.

"I'm waiting for an apology."

I looked at the clock. It was quarter past. "Look, Rosie, you're just gonna have to get used to it. I'm not a little kid anymore. I was in a place where people said things like that a hundred times a day. Worse than that! I can't just switch back to the wimp I was two years ago."

She glared at me. "Being polite is being a wimp? And tell me what you need to take a shower for if you're going up there to dig graves?"

"None of your business!" I shouted. I wanted to get out. I didn't want to be late.

"Hot water costs money!" she shouted back. "You take a shower only when you need one!"

But I was going out the door. Mrs. Dullea was on the side of the fence, her arms moving back and forth with a rake. She must have heard Rosie and me shouting. She looked up at me in an embarrassed way.

"Hi," I said.

"Hi," she said.

Then I started to laugh and I laughed all the way up to the cemetery, running through the path in the woods, and I couldn't stop myself, even though it was sounding wild and crazy, until I got to Murworth's Tomb and saw the door ajar.

10

I just stood there, looking at her. She was Lindsay and she wasn't Lindsay. She was taller, bigger in some inexplicable way. And her face was narrower and made me think of a bird. Her hair. All her long hair was gone. It was cropped short, close to her ears, curls spilling out onto her forehead. I felt in awe, like she was a hundred years older than me. And then her face sort of broke up into half smiles and sorrows and I said, "Oh, Lin," and grabbed her, squeezing her to me.

We stayed like that for a long moment, her body giving toward mine. I could smell her, feel her, touch her, but she was a stranger. And she went rigid and pushed herself back.

"You rat," she said, striking my arm, socking me softly with silly babyish blows.

"Why am I a rat?" I asked, but she ran, out the door, into the woods, not following the path, just running blind. Branches snapped back and slapped my face as I followed. I didn't care. Let them hit me, I thought. Let them punish me for changing Lindsay into this strange woman.

I let her run herself out until she collapsed on

the ground, gasping and crying. But no tears. Crying without tears.

I sat down next to her and pulled her over. She didn't protest, just collapsed into my lap like a sack of clothes. Not like a child. She was too angular. I remembered soft curves. This Lindsay was full of angles that seemed treacherous and sharp.

"Lin, why am I a rat?"

She shrugged herself away again. "All that stuff I wrote you. I felt so stupid when you didn't answer. I felt like a real jerk."

In a minute, I thought, it will be all over. It will get straightened out. Lindsay will become the same as before. It's natural to feel a little strange after two years. Lindsay and me, growing up together—she was the only person who really liked me when I was a little kid. I met her in a mud puddle. It was raining and they were tearing up one of the streets for new sewer lines. I was coming home from school, watching myself so I wouldn't make Rosie mad by getting wet. There was Lindsay jumping up and down in a puddle. Her shoes went down with a plop and came up with a suck and a pop. She watched me avoid the puddle and she laughed. I just walked on by. And I heard her coming after me.

"Hey, you!" she shouted. "Dontcha like mud?"

I kept walking down that street, avoiding catastrophe. She grabbed my arm, leaving a big muddy handprint on my sleeve.

"It's okay," she said when she saw my horrified stare. "I'm gonna get in big trouble, too."

She told me she wasn't supposed to be walking home alone and asked me to tell her mother I brought her from school, and say she accidentally fell in a puddle. So the first time I ever met Lindsay's mother, I lied. And then I somehow got into a routine of walking Lindsay home, crossing her at Monrovia Boulevard. I let Lindsay get away with anything. She held my hand, gave me birthday presents of soggy Twinkies, and put red pepper on my trick-or-treat candy.

"I never got any letters from you, Lin," I said.

"I was so darn mad. I wrote you that first week. God, I think it was a sappy letter. I was afraid to write again. And then I got mad."

She looked at me. Her nose was red and her lip was quivering, but her eyes were dry. An accusing bird's eyes, ringed in black. Lindsay wearing eye makeup. I'd never seen that before.

"I swear it," I said, wondering why I should feel so defensive. "All I got were those cards."

"What cards?"

"Christmas, birthdays, Easter."

Lindsay made a sound like a laugh. "I'd never send any stupid Easter card."

I thought: What are we doing, after two years, having this argument about cards?

"I sent two letters right away," she was saying. "I didn't even wait for you to answer. I missed you so much!" She moved slightly away from me. "I never got a single letter from you."

"This is crazy," I said. "We're both saying the same thing. Do we believe each other?"

Lindsay ignored the question, she just went on talking, as if she were talking out a dream. "I kept writing. I was angry, but then I thought maybe they wouldn't let you send letters. So every time I'd get this feeling that you didn't give a shit, I'd tell myself that you'd write me if you could. I even felt I was being sort of magnanimous about it. And then I found out from Rosie how you were sending her letters all the time, telling her you wanted soap and socks and all that stuff. I felt really bad, Mickey."

"But I never got one letter, don't you understand?" I shouted. "So I gave up." I felt like giving up now. How was I going to make her listen?

Inside, the smirky sarcastic voice was coming on strong. *You buy that she wrote you love letters?* it asked. *She's checking you out, man, wants to see if you're worth salvaging. You remember the shape you were in when you left here? You were a twitching fart-freaking jerk-off! You couldn't even talk right. You think a girl like this was gonna write letters to a guy like that? She's just trying to cover up. It's an old trick. Make a lot of noise and nobody will notice you goofed up.*

Lindsay suddenly groaned. "Oh, God, I don't know what happened to all my letters. I wish you believed me."

"I do believe you," I said, and I wanted to like crazy.

"Let's go back," she said. She was close, taking

my hand. "Let's go back to our place. Start over,
okay?"

I was shaking as I followed her back through the
woods. She pulled my arm because I was going so
slow. She was smiling. She took jumping steps
through the dead leaves, reminding me again of the
long-ago Lindsay. It made my heart feel better. But
I felt scared. I wanted it to be the same as the past
and I knew that it had to be different.

The door of the tomb was wide open, waiting
for us like a mouth. We went inside and Lindsay
kicked it shut. We leaned against the cement base
that held the casket. She lifted her head, she closed
her eyes. I touched her lips with mine, very softly. It
was like it used to be. My Lindsay.

"Mickey, Mickey," she said, moving her mouth
against my lips, trying to push with her tongue. I felt
myself tense up. Wait. Too fast. I had to get used to
all this again. I had to get things in order.

"It's been so long," she said in a voice all husky,
it sort of embarrassed me. I couldn't get my mind
and body to work together. I kept thinking I wanted
to go on kissing her, touching her, but I felt like a
lump of ice.

Her hands were moving up and down my back,
inside my jacket, pulling at my shirt. Incongruously,
I had a vision of Freegull looking at his dirty magazines, saying, "Oh, God, I can't stand it!"

"Lindsay, not here," I said. "We can't do anything here."

She just murmured against me.

I thought I heard a noise outside. I tried to tell her. "Listen, Lin, what if somebody comes along?" This was all too quick, too unplanned.

You're an idiot, the voice in my head said with scorn. *Worse than that, you're a virgin. Worse than that, you can't even get an erection.*

"What's the matter?" Lindsay said, as if coming out of a trance. "What's wrong? Why are you acting this way? You're making me feel stupid! Why didn't you just tell me you didn't want me anymore? Why'd you have to let me act like such a jerk!"

There was the noise again, a scraping at the door. A thin shaft of light struck across the tomb floor, missing us by only an inch.

"Michael? Lindsay? You in there?"

Lindsay pulled away from me and her hands flapped at her hair, trying to smooth it, and wiped at her lips.

The light poured over us. Aunt Heva's shape filled the doorway. She was leaning on a cane and looked just like a witch from a fairy tale.

"I thought I'd find you here," Aunt Heva said.

Lindsay turned to escape, looking like a lightning bug trapped in a mayonnaise jar. "I hate you!" she cried as she pushed away from me and rushed past Aunt Heva.

My knees gave out and I crumpled down and sat on the cold stone floor. I didn't need to do any fixing up. Aunt Heva could see, my fly was zipped.

I put my head down in my hands. I was aware that Aunt Heva was standing over me. After a time she put out her hand and I took it, feeling her dry, leathery witch's skin.

"Things change, childhood ends," she said. "Come on, Linny's waiting to show you how to work the backhoe."

"Okay," I heard myself say in a voice like a sob.

I kept wondering. When Lindsay said, "I hate you," who was she talking to?

PART

II

11

The air is fishy, like the river is crawling up the middle of Main Street. My shoes make a noise on the pavement, a nighttime-walking sound all their own.

Gary's white sneakers are quieter than my L. L. Bean clunkers. Gary is tall and a little chunky, although he sucks in his gut every once in a while, when he remembers. He has a brown beard, neatly trimmed but sort of fiercely bushy. In spite of all this he's tried to acquire a Woody Allen image. He tells me he wears sneakers with everything; he even wore them with a tuxedo to some big political ball in Washington, D. C., when he was working on a newspaper there. Gary says he's been everywhere.

"But where do you come from originally, Mr. Longman?" Rosie asked him once, and Gary said, "The Midwest, Texas, L.A., you name it." Rosie didn't like that answer.

I hadn't noticed, but Gary wore his sneakers the day he came to talk to Rosie about the room. Rosie noticed. She says, "Artistic people like to have odd habits. It makes them feel important."

Gary has a lot of habits, as I suppose Rosie would call them. One is going for walks in the middle of the night, which is why we're walking down Main Street at midnight. The witching hour, he calls it. He makes jokes about ghoulies rising up from their graves and I have to tell him to cut it out. I get enough of graves in the daytime.

"So why'd you want to work in a graveyard, anyway?" Gary asks me.

"It's a job. It pays. And I didn't have to give references."

"We'll have to see about that," Gary says. "You got your GED, right? You could get something better."

Sure, right, I think, but then maybe Gary has connections. The way he talks sometimes, it seems like anything could be possible. In fact, Gary can be a very pushy person. Like when he asks me questions. He makes me feel guilty if I don't answer. He makes me feel he's doing me a favor asking me questions, so how can I refuse?

Most of the time all we do is talk about the case. Gary said he heard about it when he was working on the Canuga *Post,* and he got interested. He said lots of times, the only way the truth comes out is when a reporter decides to investigate. "I don't like to see anyone railroaded," he said.

So we talk about all aspects of what happened, so that we can get at the truth, and I try not to get upset at any of the questions.

Like the other day, he said in his car, "So they didn't send you up the river because you were a murder suspect, did you?"

Up the river. I savored it a moment. It sounded like the penitentiary. Where've you been, Michael? Up the river.

"I mean, the girl's death might have been a factor, but you were sent up for breaking and entering. How do you figure you did that?" he asked.

"I never broke in anywhere. I never stole anything."

"You went into people's houses and you didn't cooperate when they asked you why you did it. You wouldn't tell them. Are you going to tell me? Stop at the stop sign up ahead."

"I cooperated," I said, and prepared for the stop sign. Gary was teaching me how to drive. I put my foot down slowly and carefully so the car wouldn't lurch. I wanted to be able to drive smooth and cool, but the car stalled anyway.

Gary laughed—I don't know if it was because I stalled or because he didn't like my answer. I felt a little pissed at him.

"If you know so much, it wasn't breaking and entering," I told him. "It was criminal trespass."

I went too fast around a corner. Gary said, "Take it easy, you're doing fine."

You might think that Gary is a hard person to like, but he talks straight, that's all. And I talk straight back. Sometimes, though, he yells, and I have to get used to that. But now I know he's only yelling because he's excited about what he's saying, feeling it strong. He never yells when I drive, not even when it looks like I might crack up. I'd prefer an automatic so I wouldn't have all this stuff with the clutch and gears, but Gary says I'd better learn to drive a standard shift because what if I'm the lone survivor of a disaster and the only escape is a Volkswagen bug? That's one of Gary's things, saying *What if?* What if the poor people this, and what if the bomb that, and what if the President doesn't get his act together? When Gary talks politics, he yells.

I didn't really want to talk to Gary about criminal trespass. It wasn't something I was particularly proud of. If you want to know the truth, it was a thing I didn't understand very well, no matter how much Kline tried to get me to explain it. But before I knew it, I was talking about it to Gary. I was putting him in stitches about the time I was in some house and I heard somebody come in the front door. I didn't want to get caught, so I ran to the bathroom and hid behind the shower curtain. There I was, standing in the bathtub, and wouldn't you know, this guy comes into the bathroom after me. I was praying he wouldn't want to take a shower. But no, he unzips his fly and takes a leak. Time went so slow, I could count every drop. My knees were shaking. He flushed and went out. I must have waited an hour before I got the guts to leave that bathroom. I kept thinking, what if he had sat down on the can with a magazine and I had to stand behind the curtain while he took a dump? I must have laughed up the street with that when I finally sneaked out the back door. Dr. Kline didn't think it was so funny when I told him. Gary did. It's great to have somebody like him to talk to, somebody on the same wavelength. I couldn't tell Rosie or Grandpop something like that.

I admit when Gary arrived I was a little on the awestruck side. Here was a guy who was gonna spend all his time working on a book to clear me. How did I act with him? I felt beholden and I didn't know if it was possible to get friendly with a person like him. But right away Gary put me at ease. He must have even noticed that I was upset that first afternoon, after that scene with Lindsay in the tomb, because he said, "Hey, you look strung out; how about coming up to listen to some jazz?" He made instant coffee on the hot plate and he didn't ask me any questions. I sat there and I cooled out.

In one afternoon the room had changed. Gary's typewriter was on the gateleg table and there was a stack of paper and a stack of files and a big dirty mug of pens and pencils.

He had books scattered all around, lined up on the windowsill and on top of the bureau. His clothes were dumped in the middle of the bed and he made a joke about it but didn't bother to put anything away while I was there. He had a nice stereo system, graphic equalizer, expensive speakers. I bet Rosie split a gut when she saw Gary bringing speakers in.

Rosie still has not said one word about Gary writing a book. But the way she puts up with everything he does, I guess she thinks it's for a good cause. Like Gary's midnight jaunts. They make her nervous because she can't put the chain on the front door until he comes home. The house has a million windows anybody could break but Rosie worries about the chain. She gave Gary a key, of course, and the first time he went out at night she didn't know it. When he tried to get back in, the chain was on and he had to pound and wake Rosie up. Grandpop was ticked. Now Rosie can't sleep, worrying and listening for Gary to come in so she can run downstairs and barricade the house.

"That's what you get for running your home-stewed boardinghouse," Grandpop told her one morning.

"You're hard," she said. "Only an unfeeling man would throw a person's dream back in their face."

"Listen," I tell Gary now, as we go past Pandolphi's old shoe repair, where hunks of waxy cheese hang in the window like bodies. "If you can, try not to go out for walks every night. Rosie gets worried."

"Sure," Gary says. "As I get more into the book, I'll be writing at night. Now I'm working on getting the feel of the town, orienting myself. Give me another week and I'll be on a roll, typing till dawn."

Poor Rosie. I can imagine her lying there listening to the clatter of the typewriter all night long.

People are the key to the truth, Gary says. He wants to interview everybody, not only people involved with the case, but every single person in

Kornkill. "You never know what might turn up," he says.

I'm going to be more famous than ever in this town, even before the book is published. I wonder if I'll be able to buy a sandwich in the deli at lunchtime without everybody jumping under the tables because Michael the Murderer is there.

But what the heck, I can go along with it. Instead of the deli, I can bring Rosie's chicken salad sandwiches up to the cemetery. No gawkers there.

Sometimes, Aunt Heva comes out with a mug of soup for me at lunchtime, and she stands right on somebody's grave and talks to me while I drink it. "It's peaceful here," she says, wrinkling her face into the sun. So far we have not talked much about Lindsay. Aunt Heva told me that Iraleen is sick. "She's seeing a doctor in Melford, for her nerves," Aunt Heva said. I wondered if it was a hint that I shouldn't make waves by trying to see Lindsay. Somehow I don't feel like asking Aunt Heva about it. I used to think she could give advice on anything, but after her barging into Murworth's Tomb, I'm not so sure I believe her. When the mug is empty, Aunt Heva takes it and trots off, walking all over the graves.

Rosie thinks walking on a grave is a sacrilege. She gets all holy in a cemetery, whispering and blessing herself. When I was a little kid, she brought me along when she took care of Grandpop's first wife's grave, pulling weeds and planting flowers. I never knew my grandmother, so I didn't feel sad or holy. The only thing that bothered me was that half the tombstone said Alberta Thorn and the other half was blank. I wanted to know who was going on the other side. When Rosie said Grandpop's name would be chiseled in when he died, I worried where Rosie's name would go. It became one of those dopey things you ponder over when you're a kid. One day it got cleared up when I heard Rosie telling Moira that she had a plot in the Catholic cemetery in Melford. I remember a big weight getting off my chest and I ran outside and ripped my shirt climbing a tree.

Now that I'm working in the cemetery, Rosie says I can check on Bertie's grave and save her the trip. It's funny how my life suddenly revolves around the dead, when Gary is so busy pursuing the living.

We reached the bottom of Main Street. Across Railroad Avenue the station looked desolate and the sign was still hanging crooked, groaning a little in the night air. The Station Diner was closed but the red BUD sign winked at the street.

"I went in there for starters," Gary said. "Talked to everybody."

"What for?"

"Get the lay of the land," Gary said. "You find out a lot in the grass roots of a place."

I looked at him. "The Station Diner is grass roots?" I could hear Rosie's voice in my head: Stay out of that place, it's full of lowlifes.

There used to be a bunch of girls who hung out,

older than me, some of them had dropped out of high school. "Hey, Mickey Mouse!" they would yell if I walked by. Their lips were smeary with bright red lipstick and they smoked cigarettes. I felt scared and excited by them. Sometimes, I got up the courage and went in for a Coke. Wakefield and I used to sit in the back booth and slide down low in the seats and tell each other how we would like to get those girls in the sack. The diner always smelled of stale beer and fried fish.

"Only bums hang out in there," I informed Gary. "You won't get any facts from them."

I wondered if anybody had told him about me and Wakefield. "Yeah, we remember those two little dips, sipping Cokes and talking big."

"What you know about this town is ancient history, Mike," Gary said. "It's all B.C. We're talking about A.D. now. You can't judge the present from the past."

"You mean B.M., don't you?" I said, and Gary laughed.

"There's a whole new crowd hangs out here now," he said.

"How do you know what it was like B.M.?"

"I ask a lot of questions."

"So what kind of answers did you get about me?"

"Oh, I didn't talk about you," Gary replied. "I got them talking about the town, about people in general. I like to get a little town history into the book. The roots of crime interest me. Does it start in the home? In the environment?"

"Hey, wait a minute!" I said. "What are you talking about crime? I thought this whole project was to show me clear. I didn't commit any crime, if you remember."

"Stay cool," Gary said. "I was generalizing. Writing a book isn't just one single idea. You have to bring the threads together. What are you so uptight about?"

"I didn't do it."

Gary put his hand on my shoulder. "Somebody did it," he said. "So if somebody did it, and you're the one who *saw* somebody do it, what's wrong with looking for the roots of the crime?"

I relaxed. "Okay," I said. "I just didn't think of it that way. I'm a little stretched out on the subject, that's all."

We resumed walking. We went along Railroad Avenue, toward the sausage factory. I was acutely aware that somewhere above us, Monrovia Park was hanging in the darkness. But I did what Gary said. I stayed cool.

"You know, Michael, we have to talk about why you feel so responsible," Gary said.

"Me?"

"Yeah, you. I get the feeling you're fighting the fact that you didn't do it. I get the feeling sometimes you think you did do it!"

"I get the feeling this is all bullshit," I told him.

"I saw a man push a woman off the wall. Everybody thinks I'm lying."

Gary must have heard the edge on my voice, I didn't try to disguise it. "Okay, all right," he said, and dropped the subject.

We walked along without saying anything. I felt bad. I didn't want to fight with Gary, but I didn't want him trying to mix me up, either. I'd had enough of the psychoanalysis game with Kline and Painter.

"What do you have, a tape recorder in your brain?" I asked to lighten things up. "How do you remember everything people tell you?"

"Practice," Gary said, but his voice was preoccupied. "Shhhhh," he said, stopping in his tracks. "What's going on over there?"

Whatever it was, I wasn't interested. But Gary's beard was already jutting forward, his nose following, his whole body poised like a bird dog on the scent.

We were standing on the edge of the marshy ground that sticks out into the river like a shaggy finger. In the summer it smells bad, but now it had a sort of homey odor, like a familiar musty closet.

"I don't see anything," I said. The yellowy streetlights were behind us, there wasn't much moon. Far beyond the marsh the river glimmered faintly.

Then something was coming toward us. A girl. Somebody must have driven their car out onto the mushy ground and got stuck. Asshole thing to do.

The girl was listing like a sinking ship and even from far away I could hear her feet squishing and popping in the muck.

All of a sudden I realized that I had been waiting to bump into Lindsay all night. I had been hoping, somehow, that we would meet up with her on the street. I could introduce her to Gary, drop a hint about who he was. What a crazy idea. As if Lindsay's mother would let her out this late on a school night.

It was a half-assed wish and now I was afraid it was going to come true. I was afraid this girl coming across the marsh was Lindsay and that I'd have to look again into those black-ringed, accusing eyes.

And I was afraid to find out that maybe she had been out on a date, with the jerk whose car was stuck.

I was afraid, I was afraid, I was afraid. What else was new?

12

It wasn't Lindsay. It was a girl all dressed up, and her high-heeled shoes and ankles were covered with mud. She didn't seem too happy to see us. She was probably embarrassed.

The streetlight threw off enough of a measly light so that I could tell her face was familiar. Who? Gary was making sympathetic noises and helping her get out of the muck. But I just stood there, wondering who she was.

"What are you staring at?" she asked me. She had a funny voice, tentative and fragile, like it might give out any minute. Maybe because she was upset and wanted to cry because her boyfriend messed up their date.

"Can we help?" Gary was asking.

"Mary Ann," I said.

"So?" She was looking at me like I was something for sale and not worth the price. "God," she said. "It's you."

"That's me, good old God."

She smiled, then her smile vanished. "Pete's car is sinking. You know Pete Wheaton?" Her expression showed what she thought of him. She gestured in an offhand way. "You want to help him? He needs a tow truck."

Out on the marsh the wheels were spinning. A disembodied voice floated toward us. "Awww, fuck!"

"We could give a push," Gary said. I thought of his white sneakers. I thought of my L. L. Beans. I thought of Rosie's carpets.

Gary was already picking his way out to the car. Mary Ann shrugged and followed. I brought up the rear, trying not to get my shoes dirty.

"It's hopeless," Mary Ann said. Pete Wheaton was hanging out the car window, watching his tires spin. I remembered him vaguely; he'd been ahead of me in school. Gary went over to give him advice.

"So, how're you doing?" Mary Ann asked me.

"I'm okay," I said.

Gary yelled that we should all push. Mary Ann gave a soft snort of a laugh and stepped away. Gary and I pushed and Pete gave it the gas and stalled the car.

"Oh, forget it," said Mary Ann. Her words were so strong, but her voice was so frail. I'd never noticed that before. But then I hadn't noticed her much at all after our first fleeting friendship in sixth grade, those months after Ginger McKee's death.

"Heave!" Gary ordered. I felt like my arms were going to snap, and sweat broke out all over my head. I was about to echo Mary Ann's sentiments— forget it—when the car leaped forward out of the deep ruts the tires had made. Pete let out a whoop and kept going in a wide arc. He didn't even stop as Mary Ann grabbed the door and jumped in. They drove off the marsh and bounced onto Railroad Avenue, Pete driving like he would never stop again.

"You're welcome," Gary said in an offended voice.

"A little grass roots," I reminded him.

We walked back up Main Street. Gary began expounding on one of his political what-ifs, but I didn't listen. I was thinking how Mary Ann hadn't asked anything except how was I doing.

How was I doing?

Right now I was tired. For once I agreed with Rosie, I should be convalescing. All day digging graves, all night stalking the streets and acting like Superman. Besides that, my shoes were encased in five inches of mud.

We were on the last lap home when we met up with Charlie Melville. His banana boat came sneaking up behind us.

"That you, Thorn?" he growled, like I was some monster who shouldn't be on the streets.

"Yeah," I said. No use to deny it.

"Whatta you think you're doing?"

"Taking a walk." I felt the panic button go off inside me. I shivered. The hot sweat of the marsh turned cold and clammy on my head.

"It's all right, Officer," Gary said in a bright voice, his best pushy, know-it-all voice. "He's with me."

"That so?" Melville said.

"As far as I know, we are within our rights to take a walk on the streets of this town," Gary said. His head was cocked to one side, leaning down a bit to speak to Melville, smiling a little, looking confident.

"It's two o'clock in the morning," Melville said.

"I don't see that time makes any difference," said Gary.

"Who're you?" Melville asked, sticking his head out the window to get a better look.

"Gary Longman. I'm a journalist." Like a smug toad, Charlie Melville sat, unimpressed. Gary's smile faded. "I don't see why we should be subjected to this questioning."

"You two going home now?" Melville asked, ignoring Gary's remarks.

"Yes we are, but—"

The banana boat just slid away, cutting Gary in midsentence.

"I don't believe it!" he said. "Who does that jerk think he is?"

I could see Gary wasn't used to cops. Gary might know a lot, but he didn't have a clue about how the other half lives.

"Stay cool," I told him. "That's the way it is. Once you've been caught, they keep trying to catch you again."

13

The ironic thing is that although I was in Monrovia Park the night of the murder and had reported the murder myself, the cops didn't think of me as a suspect until they caught me on the criminal trespass charge. Only after that did they start grilling me about the murder. So I told them again, I'd seen a man push the girl off the top of the wall. They didn't believe me. They said they had an eyewitness willing to swear I was alone in the park that night.

I got scared when they said that. I wondered why anybody would lie and say it was me who did it. Sitting in the room at the police station, hearing about the eyewitness, that was when I first got the feeling in my throat. Like it was closing up, going dry as a desert, and all I could get out was a few scratchy croaks. They gave me a glass of water and the feeling went away.

Rosie and Grandpop were scared, too. I kept telling them it wasn't true, but I began to feel hopeless. It didn't seem to matter what the truth was, I was going to get blamed for the murder.

I wanted to know who the eyewitness was, but nobody would tell me. They can keep a lot of stuff from you when you're a kid, I guess. Maybe if I'd had one of those hotshot lawyers like on television, things would have been different. But I got somebody from Legal Aid, and then Grandpop broke down and said he'd pay for Gilbert Passone, who mostly drew up wills and went to real estate closings. He didn't know shit about murder.

But then something happened with the eyewitness's testimony, and the pressure was suddenly off. They dropped the murder business and started hassling me for the criminal trespass, although whenever they got a chance, they'd drop dark hints about my involvement with the murder. They couldn't prove anything but they were still hanging it over my head.

When I told all this to Gary, including the raw deal with Gilbert Passone, who was as good as useless in juvenile court, Gary said something that really surprised me. He said I was taking that same old line all criminals took, that they were screwed by the courts and their lawyers, when they knew they were guilty. So I asked him how that could apply to me, since I was *not* guilty.

"They did catch you on Willow Street, didn't they? Sitting in the living room? You were guilty of that."

"I didn't need two years at the school for sitting in a living room!"

"You screwed yourself," Gary said, "because you were uncooperative."

"And how was I uncooperative?" I yelled back at him.

"You wouldn't talk!"

"I couldn't," I told him. "There's a difference."

Something happened to my voice and I didn't have any control over it. That feeling I first got in the police station kept coming back. Rosie would say, "What? what?" and tell me to speak up, stop mumbling. Grandpop got mad at the dinner table because I was grunting. I was clearing my throat, I told him. But I had to clear my throat a million times a day and it was still clogged up. Rosie made me gargle. They sent me to the doctor for antibiotics. All the time I was gargling and popping pills, I knew it wasn't any infection. It was like some force inside of me, putting my voice to sleep.

"What beats me," Gary said, getting sympathetic again, "is why they didn't get a psychiatrist to diagnose it. Hundreds of kids develop problems like that when they're in a traumatic situation like a courtroom. They stutter or go mute. Some of them even have epileptic seizures."

It's too late now, but it makes me feel better to hear it.

They kept asking me *why* so much, I just couldn't tell them anything anymore. Why did I have to go into people's houses? What was I after since I didn't steal anything? Gary also wanted to know why. "Think about it," he said. "It's an important point for the book."

The feeling just came over me, a few days after

that night in Monrovia Park. I couldn't get that night out of my mind, it kept playing itself over and over like a bad dream. I kept seeing that mess at the bottom of the wall, looking like somebody had thrown their old clothes out a window. It was hard to take in, that a human being could look so much like a heap of old clothes. A totally insane idea flashed in my head: that I could scoop everything up and take it to the dry cleaners and the girl would be returned good as new, cleaned and pressed, hung up on a hanger and covered with a plastic bag. I went running out of the park, and even as I punched 911 on the pay phone near the gates, I kept thinking I should be calling One-Hour Martinizing instead.

I couldn't concentrate on anything. I got the jitters and couldn't sit still in school. Rosie said, "Stay home, you've been through a lot, rest and take it easy." So one afternoon I was just walking through Kornkill, trying to walk the jitters off.

All of a sudden I got this compulsion that I had to go into one of the houses on the street. I had to do it. I had some vague notion that I would find something out, but it was more of a gut-urge, not an idea I considered sensibly.

It just happened that the first house I picked was empty and the side door unlocked. I don't know what I would have done if someone had been home, because I didn't plan it, I just opened the door and walked in. Sometimes, I used to think it was fated that I didn't get caught on the first try, and it set everything up to happen again. If I'd been caught that first time, I probably would have chickened out.

Rosie has this thing called fate, the answer to anything you can't explain. For her it's closely tied up with God's will. "I was walking past Pasek's and I felt this urge to go inside and they were having a one-day special on pork loin," she'll say. "It was as if I was guided by the Almighty. And I saved sixty cents a pound!" Rosie and God get together for all kinds of practical stuff like that. In the middle of the mess with the court Rosie said, "There's a reason for everything, Mickey." So far I haven't discovered the reason for what I did. Maybe God wanted to give me a little experience, thinking I was leading this cushy life and needed a shock.

So, okay, nobody was home. I had no idea whose house it was. It smelled nice, like baking apple pies. The kitchen was early American with a collection of frying pans going up the wall like a staircase. There must have been ten of them, starting with a tiny one and ending up with a monster, all in a graduated row. On the kitchen counter was a piece of meat wrapped in plastic, defrosting. It was sweating a pool of pale blood. I looked at it and got out of the kitchen fast.

I went into the bathroom and looked in the medicine chest. You can tell a lot about people by looking in the medicine chest. I counted two bottles of aspirin and two bottles of Bufferin and about ten different prescriptions in the brown plastic containers you get from Happy's Drugs. I thought of mixing the pills up, sticking aspirin in the prescription container and vice versa, but I knew that was a sick joke and somebody could die. It was a passing thought, not even formulated. I would never do a thing like that.

But I was a little nervous that I even had such a passing thought, so I got out of the bathroom. In the bedroom was a double bed covered with a satin comforter. I thought of the sickly owner of the house, tossing and turning in that bed at night, getting up to take aspirin and Bufferin and ten different kinds of pills. I looked under the bed and found dust balls. There were never any dust balls under Rosie's beds.

I walked around real quiet, on tiptoe. I spent some time in the living room, sitting on the couch, trying to figure what kinds of conversations took place there, trying to fathom what it was I needed to know. I don't think I really worried about being caught. I felt relaxed sitting on the couch. But after a while it felt like a boring room. This isn't what I want, I remember thinking to myself.

As I passed through the kitchen again, to go out the side door, I saw the meat. I gave it a shove and it fell with a soft thud into the sink. I think that's when I first had an inkling that I could actually do something in the houses, not just look. Pushing the meat into the sink was not like changing pills. The owner would think it fell in by itself. No big deal.

I walked out of the house and nobody noticed me.

"So you weren't all innocence and light," Gary said to me. "You didn't steal anything maybe, but you tampered. Was it all a big joke to you?"

"I was in shock, remember?" I said. "What seems like a joke now might not have been a joke then."

"Sure," Gary said. "Listen, I understand."

It beats me if I can latch on to the purpose of it all now. The answer stays there, like it always did, just beyond range, beckoning me with a bony hand, then giving me the finger when I get too close.

In the gab sessions in Gary's room at night, I don't mind telling him things. It's a different atmosphere from having a session at the school. Gary makes coffee, he has deli sandwiches in his refrigerator. He heats up old pizza in his toaster oven. Rosie would have a fit about the toaster oven, so I warned Gary and he hides it now. The boarder is supposed to do light cooking only, on the two hot-plate rings that sit on top of the half-size fridge. Dishwashing is done in the bathroom sink. Boarders are supposed to eat regular meals out, in a restaurant in town. It's the big bone of contention between Rosie and Grandpop. She would like to run a regular establishment, with meals for boarders. But Grandpop says he won't have any g.d. hotel guest sitting at the table with him three times a day.

When I tell Gary about stuff I did in the houses, it's like I'm talking about somebody else, some dumb kid, not me.

I did things like switch people's clothes around

in the bedroom bureaus. I put the woman's clothes in the man's drawers and vice versa. Once I moved the furniture around in a living room. I made everything a mirror image. It was sort of funny. Imagine coming home and finding your living room in reverse. I can laugh now and even Gary gives a chuckle. But then, I did it humorlessly. I was diligent and very serious.

The prosecutor at the hearing went on about how I affected people's nerves, gave them shocks. All I did was alter reality a little.

One time I seriously asked Dr. Kline if a person could have a heart attack because he found his wife's underwear in his sock drawer.

"The couple might lose trust in each other," he said. "Their marriage could be destroyed, even if you thought it was a practical joke."

"All because of underwear? Marriage must be crazy."

Dr. Kline shook his head at me and lit his pipe. "You tell me what you know about marriage."

"I've never been married." It was a joke, but Kline was deathly serious.

"Your grandfather's marriage, your mother's marriage."

"Grandpop spends a lot of time with his bugs. Rosie spends a lot of time in the kitchen. When they get together, they argue. I don't know a thing about my mother's marriage. How could I? I was too little. My father ran away, my mother died. The end."

"Who told you about your parents?"

I shrugged. I honestly didn't remember any specific conversations. I supposed it was Rosie. It sort of siphoned down through the years.

"One of those things you can't remember," I said to Dr. Kline.

"We can remember everything," he said. "But sometimes we don't want to."

All this I told to Gary.

"Enough about Dr. Kline," Gary said. "Tell me about the school itself. Did you make any friends there?"

"You gotta be kidding."

"Come on. Not everybody could have been a Freegull."

I remember sitting in a group meeting and this kid said he had changed at the school. "When I came here, I was fucked up," he said. "I didn't trust nobody jackshit. Now I'm willing to give it a chance. I see you all got your problems, too, you know? I think you are all like . . ." He stopped and got red in the face but the leader said he should go on, so he sputtered, "you are like my brothers."

I got the creeps when he said that. I looked around the room and I couldn't see anybody I'd feel like a brother to.

The only kid I felt anything for was the wimp. They called him Oliver Twist and yelled, "More, please," every time they knocked him down and he cried. His name was Andrew Bartlett III, and that was a mark against him right away. I used to think he was pretty wimpy myself, but one time I was walking in the grove behind the laundry building and I heard crying and there was Bartlett sitting on the ground, bawling his head off. I thought maybe he was hurt, but I backed off when I heard him saying, "Mama, Mama, Mama." The poor little shit.

One day I asked Kline what Bartlett was in for. Kline didn't want to tell me at first, but then he shrugged his shoulders in his "what the hell" way. He was always doing that and breaking the rules. "His father killed his mother," Kline said. "And Andrew tried to kill his father when he saw what he'd done."

I got a horrible knot in my gut and was sorry I'd asked. But all this I didn't tell Gary. I said, sure, there were a couple of regular guys but nobody close.

Gary rocked back in his chair.

"I'm bushed," he said. "I think that's all for tonight."

I felt it was wrong for him to decide when we should stop talking, as if he was in charge. I'd had enough of that with Kline and Painter. I got up to leave, but it seemed like things were off balance. I was cooperating with Gary, telling him everything, and it bothered me. Sure, he was teaching me how to drive, that was nice, except the whole time he was teaching me, he was also asking questions. The old smirker inside my head kept saying: *Hey, Mr. Nice Guy, you deserve something in return.*

"Listen, Gary," I said, hesitating at the door. "Could you do me a favor?"

"Sure thing, what is it?"

"Could you find something out for me? I want to know if the school had rules about getting letters, whether they could censor them so they wouldn't get through."

Gary perked up. He wanted to know what letters and from who.

"I'd tell you about it, but like you said, it's late. But if you could just find out what they might have done with the letters, I'd really appreciate that."

"I'll see what I can do," he said. "I'll try."

"Thanks." His curiosity was breaking out on him like a sweat, he wanted to know more. What was I doing, playing a game? It wasn't fair. I had to stop thinking that Gary was like Dr. Kline or Dr. Painter. So I added, "This girl I know said she sent me a bunch of letters. I never got any of them. I just want to know what happened."

Gary pounced on this. "Good idea!" he said enthusiastically. "We'll find out if she's lying!"

"Thanks," I said, and shut the door, feeling a little weak. Lying—that was so blunt. Gary got right to the point, so what was I upset about? Wasn't that what I wanted, too?

But now that I'd asked him, I almost wished I hadn't. If he told me Lindsay sent the letters, I'd be glad. But if he told me she didn't, what was I going to do then?

Still, I felt like I had taken some action, and that felt good. If I was ever going to get things straight with Lindsay, I needed some facts. After I had them, well, I'd take it from there, I supposed.

14

I was feeling good the next morning. The sun was shining like crazy and it was Indian summer in October. When I went out to bring the trash cans in for Rosie, the air smelled like anything was possible. I thought: There's a whole world out there and I don't have to stay in Kornkill forever. I felt so good all of a sudden, I didn't even care if I never found that man in the park. For the first time since I'd come back from the school, I was relaxed and content.

We were having breakfast when I heard the clunk of the mail coming through the brass slot in the front door. Rosie got up and went out to collect it. Grandpop stirred his coffee and said, "More bills."

But when Rosie came back, her face was clouded. She was trying to read through a sealed envelope and she held it up to the kitchen window to get a better view. "Open the damn thing up, why don't you?" Grandpop said.

"It's for Michael," she told him. Grandpop and I looked at each other and laughed.

Rosie handed me the envelope reluctantly and

right away I could see why, because it was something official. I stopped laughing and ripped the flap
with my thumb. A crisp folded letter fell out onto my
plate and began soaking up leftover egg yolk. Rosie
grabbed a sponge, but I pushed her arm away. I
unfolded the eggy letter and began to read. Rosie
and Grandpop were silent.

Time ticked away in a sort of noisy quiet. The
refrigerator hummed, the screen door rattled a little
in the breeze, and even as I read, I thought it was
about time to get the storm windows out of the attic,
even if it was so warm.

Gary came down the stairs from the third floor.
Wearing his sneakers, because you could hardly
hear his tread. But his whistle was loud enough and
he banged the door as he went out. Gone to talk to
the grass roots, I thought.

"Well, what is it?" Rosie finally screeched.

When I didn't answer, she turned to Grandpop.
"It's nothing. His official release, probably. It takes
a while to process. . . ."

Grandpop said, "What are you airing your
mouth for?"

I felt the blood slowly come back to my hands,
warming them up again. I felt my face tingle. "It's
okay," I said, and my voice was weak. I cleared my
throat. "Just follow-up junk. I'm supposed to see a
caseworker. Tell him if I got a job and stuff."

I was supposed to have gone weeks ago. The
papers were still upstairs in the desk drawer where
I'd shoved them when I first came home. I'd forgot-

ten. It just slipped my mind. Dr. Kline's face leered in my mind for a second. Yeah, well. I wanted to forget. This reminder was a bad taste in my mouth.

Grandpop and Rosie started breathing easy again. Rosie's cup rattled as she took it over to the sink. Grandpop sat in his chair longer than usual after the plates were cleared away. I think maybe his legs were shaky.

We'd all been scared, maybe for different reasons, but one thing was for sure—none of us wanted to be bugged by the law anymore.

When Grandpop went upstairs, Rosie said, "I heard Mr. Longman go out. He's not giving you a lesson today?"

"Maybe later," I said. "I gotta go to work anyway."

Rosie looked like she had something on her mind, so before she could bug me, I said I would be sure to do the chores and I would get the storm windows down from the attic.

She waved her hand. "No, no, you've been a good boy, Mickey." Her face had gone pink and she was looking at the floor. "I wanted to say, I'm glad about the driving lessons. When you get your license, you can take me shopping at the mall."

She said it and looked shocked that she had. Scared, too, like she thought I would tell her no way was I taking her shopping. I felt sort of bad and sad at the same time. What poor Rosie didn't know was that driving her to the mall was the one idea that had got me through the first day home.

"Hey," I said casually. "No sweat. It's a great idea. We can stock up and I won't break my back carrying six-packs home."

Rosie blushed even darker red and turned to the sink, where she began to scrub the dishes, splattering water. I left her to it, but before I went out the kitchen door, she said in a conspiratorial whisper: "Maybe we can get Pop to let you have the car."

Grandpop's old Mercedes had been languishing in the garage for years. He didn't like to drive because of his eyes. Rosie could never learn to drive, no matter how hard her friend Moira tried to teach her.

I gave Rosie the thumbs-up. I felt good again. Rosie could give me a pain in the neck, but she deserved some credit, too. She'd done some good things.

So, it's not so bad, I told myself as I crunched through the leaves up the path to the cemetery. After having traveled this way for two weeks, I no longer had any bad associations with Lindsay and that day at the tomb. What I really needed to do was put Lindsay on the back burner, as Gary would say. She could keep warm there until Gary found out about the letters. Then I would take it as it came. Whatever.

It wasn't so bad. The sun was shining. I would go to see this caseworker, P. K. Barnes. I would tell him I had a job as a caretaker at the cemetery. That sounded good. I had nothing to hide. I was clean. I didn't do drugs, no drinking except beer, I didn't even smoke cigarettes. I was pure as the driven snow; I was a saint, for crying out loud.

It suddenly occurred to me that I could now go into the Station Diner and order a beer. I hadn't even realized it before. Gary was right, I was living in B.C. Ha! No more Cokes in the back booth. When Wakefield came home for vacation we would go down there and celebrate and maybe we'd even get those chicks in bed.

For a moment I remembered that I hadn't called Wakefield back. What was I going to say? Wait till Gary finished the book, then I'd have something to say.

I felt good all morning. I had my Thermos of coffee and Rosie's sandwiches. I waved to Aunt Heva when she came out to sit on the porch. There were no graves to dig, so I raked more leaves which were falling everywhere and I trimmed the grass that had started to come up again, thinking it was spring.

Lunchtime, Aunt Heva didn't come out with soup. I sat over on the grove end, near Mary Owen's grave that Aunt Heva had said was haunted. Linny's explanation had been right, there was a huge beech tree shadowing the grave. Somebody had tied a red ribbon on a bunch of plastic flowers and stuck them in a mason jar full of water. People were nuts.

I was feeling comfortable. Graveyards are peaceful places. I mean, I might not want to sleep in one on Halloween, but on a sunny afternoon there's nothing scary. I could see how Linny could get used to fixing up dead bodies. If you did anything long enough, you got used to it. I sat there thinking the kind of comfortable thoughts you get when your mind isn't pressed about anything, although every once in a while the idea of the appointment with the caseworker in Melford put a damper on things. But anyway, I was enjoying my tuna sandwich, glad it wasn't chicken salad again. I was even going to eat all my limp carrots. Then something put its hands on my neck and I jumped a mile.

"Surprise," a voice said. Hands clamped my eyes. "Guess who?"

Lindsay. "Who?" I said. My heart had started to jump.

"I'm disappointed in you, Michael." She took her hands away. "How soon we forget," she said melodramatically.

"I never forgot," I said, but I could see she wasn't being serious. I tried to smile. I was glad, but feeling strange. Sheepish about what had happened in the tomb. Furtively, I wrapped my limp carrot sticks back up in the foil, but she grabbed it.

"What've you got? I'm starving." She looked at the carrots and made a face; started eating them anyway. "What are you? A health-food nut?"

"What are you doing here, Lin?" I asked.

"Came to see you, what else? I cut out."

"You cut school?"

"Oh oh, bad girl." Her eyes teased and mocked.

"Lin, you're gonna get in trouble."

"Oh, Michael, since when are you such an angel?"

Lindsay was sitting right next to me. I could almost feel her. Smell her scent, light and spicy off her hair. I remembered her long hair, the way it used to get into my mouth and eyes. I felt sorry it was gone. For a minute I thought if only she'd still had her long hair, things would be all right.

I wanted to reach out and touch her. I could picture myself touching her. But I sat there, keeping my hands to myself, feeling awkward.

"So, how do you like your new career?" she was asking, laughing. "You want me to ask my uncle if he'll give you a promotion?"

I felt easier. Touched her hand.

"Remember how we used to try to see the bodies? You know what I used to wonder about? If Uncle Linny kissed the females! It was one of my big erotic childhood fantasies, thinking of Uncle Linny down in the cellar with a naked woman. I used to think Aunt Heva would sneak down to spy through the keyhole."

Lindsay and me used to go down to the cellar to get the preserves for Aunt Heva. It was crystal clear in my mind, the big iron door. "There was no keyhole," I said.

Lindsay slipped her hand out from under mine. "I wasn't trying to have a big deep conversation about it," she said. "It was for fun, you know, ha ha, a joke? Why are you acting like such a drip?"

"I'm sorry, Lin."

"I'm sorry, Lin," she mimicked. Her eyes were hurt. We sat there, staring at the ground. What was wrong with us?

"I'm sorry about what happened in the tomb," I said.

"Forget it," she snapped, but her face softened.

I decided to get it into the open. "I heard your mother doesn't want me to see you. That's why I haven't been around."

"God, you really are a goody-goody," she said. Her face twisted with sadness and pain. "My mother's flipping out."

"I didn't know what to do. I didn't want to make problems."

"Sure," she said. "You don't want to make problems. What are you going to do, go through life not making problems?"

She wanted to sound angry, but her voice was tight with held-back tears. I didn't know how to answer. "I don't know why you're so mad at me, Lin," I said, sounding like a wimp.

"You don't know why I'm mad? You made me feel like a real asshole, that's why. I don't even know how you feel about me anymore. I probably shouldn't have bothered to come up here. You're right. I shouldn't have cut school."

I heard the plea in her voice, wanting me to tell her I cared, that I loved her. Take her in my arms, kiss her doubts away. All of that. The only right thing to do if I really wanted a relationship with Lindsay. But I just sat there, unable to do it. For two years I had been hanging on to this dream. And now I didn't know this person at all. I'd have to see, get to know her again, then I could decide whether there was something there or not. But how could I explain all that to her when she was sitting there, looking so vulnerable, so needing?

"It's not you, Lin. It's me."

"What's you?" She fished around in her big canvas bag and pulled out a pack of cigarettes and a lighter. She offered me the pack. I shook my head. She stuck a cigarette into her mouth and flicked the lighter. She blew smoke out of her nose. I looked away. It *is* me, I thought. I'm the one who's wrong for expecting Lindsay to have been suspended in time.

"I'm just different," I said, trying to explain. "I guess I changed." She looked at me. For a moment, behind her eyes, I think she understood that time had taken us away from each other. But then her eyes clouded over, became dark with anger.

"You're not kidding you've changed," she said, flicking ashes with nervous taps of her finger. "For all I know, something's really wrong with you. You were in the boys' school so long, maybe you've gone queer."

"Stop, Lin," I said. She kept talking, her voice racing.

"I heard it can happen. You just don't like girls anymore. The least you could do is come out and admit it like a man." She gave a shrill fake laugh and stubbed her cigarette into the grass.

"Shut up, Lin."

"It's true, isn't it? Why don't you admit it?"

I got up and walked away. I grabbed the rake and started stabbing the earth, tearing at the grass.

"Oh, damn," I heard her say. "I guess I'm a shit, huh?" She was behind me. I could smell cigarette smoke on her.

"I am, I know it. I'm sorry. It's not easy for me to say that, but I'm saying it to you. I'm sorry, Michael!" She shouted it, then lowered her voice. "I really am. My mother's making me crazy."

I stopped raking.

"She keeps worrying about you like you're Dracula. It doesn't make any sense. Daddy made her go to a psychiatrist, can you believe it? My father suggesting my mother see a shrink! I'm like a prisoner, I can't go anywhere, can't do anything because she's afraid I'll see you. And Daddy's just as bad, he says if your mother is worried about Michael she must have good reason. Then he just goes out and does his own thing. And when he comes back, all they do is fight."

"I'm sorry, Lin. I didn't know it was so bad."

My heart was banging in my chest again. I reached for her and she wound her arms around my neck and I kissed her and tasted tobacco.

"Look, I can sneak out." She giggled against my ear. "We can go back to Murworth's, our favorite motel."

I wanted to want to, but I couldn't. I took her

arms and unwound them and pushed her back from me.

"Sorry, Lin, I can't," I started to say. I meant to go on, to tell her it wasn't her fault. It wasn't her fault for growing up, for two years' worth of change. It was me, all me.

But she looked into my face and whatever she thought she saw there, it was something she couldn't take. A mask came down, hard and cold, but tears glittered in her eyes.

"You paranoid fag!" she said to me, and ran off across the graveyard, her bag banging against her side, her feet stumbling on the misinformed autumn grass.

15

Rosie was in the kitchen as usual. I slogged in and rinsed out my Thermos and put it on the drainboard to dry. I sat down at the table and stared into space, feeling whacked out.

Rosie was fixing lamb stew for dinner. The smell of searing meat filled the room. She was busy tossing chunks of it into the pot and pushing them around with a big long cooking fork.

"Take some iced tea," she said, waving the fork at the refrigerator. "The weather made me feel like summer."

But I just sat there, I didn't feel like iced tea. I stared at Rosie's latest paperback on the table, a folded paper napkin marking her place. On the cover a woman clutched a cloak around her and a man rode behind her on a big horse, leering. In the background was a gloomy-looking castle. Rosie always read historical romances. She learned bits and pieces of history from them and she would produce these tidbits at odd times, a sort of Rosie-type one-upmanship. Grandpop ignored them, but probably lots of people were impressed. The funny thing was it helped me a lot when I was a kid, doing my history homework.

"You look down in the dumps," she said as she put the cover on the big iron pot and turned down the gas.

"I'm just tired," I said. "Did you know Iraleen's going to a shrink in Melford?"

I could see it was news to Rosie. She sat down across from me, still holding the fork. "Imagine," she said.

"Why do you think she needs a shrink?"

"Well, how would I know?"

We both pondered for a few moments, turning it over in our minds. I hoped Rosie wouldn't say that Iraleen was so scared of me she was going out of her mind. I didn't believe that myself.

"She always was high strung," Rosie said at last. "I suppose it's getting worse with age. And her husband doesn't help."

"What's the matter with him?"

"Questions, questions, do you think I know everybody's business?" Rosie got up again to check on the stew, to stall for time. She didn't know whether what she knew was proper for my ears, I could tell the signs. Somewhere between sprinkling the garlic powder and cutting an onion, Rosie made up her mind. "Boyd Johnson's a run-around. He always was. She knew that before she married him. Her 'Johnny' she always called him." Rosie clamped her lips shut. "I shouldn't be saying this to you."

I laughed. I felt cheered up for the first time

since Lindsay's visit this afternoon. "Oh, come on, I'm not a kid anymore. Didn't you run around before you married Grandpop?"

Rosie looked mock-shocked. "The truth was I had planned to remain a maiden lady. I took care of my parents, God rest their souls, and I never expected to marry. I gave up on it."

"You didn't answer the question," I told her. She prodded me with the fork. "Get yourself washed up."

Iraleen's visits to a shrink probably had nothing to do with me at all, even if Lindsay said her mother had been scared since I came home. Lindsay talked a lot of rubbish these days. I couldn't believe everything she said. Which reminded me.

"Is Gary back?"

"Gary!" Rosie made a face. "You spend more time in his room than your own."

"I like to talk to him, okay?"

"He's been out all day. I wish you'd spend time with people your own age."

"I have to talk to Gary if we're going to find out the truth."

Rosie frowned. "Truth about what?"

I felt disgusted with Rosie. "What happened in Monrovia Park, that's about what!"

Rosie looked so shocked, I calmed down. "Well, what did you think we talked about? He's here to write a book on it, isn't he?"

"For heaven's sake!" Rosie began hacking the onions into little pieces.

"Did you really think it was a big dark secret? I'm the hero of the book! Did you think he was going to make everything up in his head, like one of these stupid books you read?"

I gave her paperback a shove and it fell off the table. Rosie stopped chopping the onions to death and looked at the book lying on the floor. I went around to pick it up. That was a cheap shot I shouldn't have taken.

"Look, Rosie," I said. "Gary has to talk to me about what happened, just like he has to talk to everybody else."

"Everybody else? Who?"

"Anybody who knows anything. Even you and Grandpop."

Rosie blanched. "Oh, no. I don't want any interviews. Your grandfather wouldn't stand for it." She put the knife down and wiped at her eyes. "The onions," she said, seeing I was upset she was crying. She sat down again, sagged down, as if she was never going to get up again. "Oh, what have I done?"

"If you feel like this, I don't know why you ever let him come here," I said. I was honestly perplexed.

"It's hard to explain, Mickey. I thought you deserved a better chance than you had. We both know Pop is a tightwad, no, I'll say it out loud. I thought Mr. Longman's book would help you. But somehow I never expected you to be involved. I don't suppose I thought it through properly. I don't know anything about writing books."

Rosie was a dichotomy. She believed I was innocent and she believed I was guilty. That's how it was with her. Maybe Dr. Kline would call her a split personality. Maybe she'd invited Gary to come and write the book as much for herself as for me. If Gary could come up with the answer in black and white, she'd know what to believe. Once and for all she could get rid of her doubts.

I didn't hate her or anything. I think I was getting philosophical. I found myself getting up and opening the refrigerator and taking out the glass bottle of iced tea. I poured a glass for Rosie and one for myself.

We drank the tea in silence. And when her glass was empty, Rosie pulled herself out of her chair and went back to the stew. And I took the glasses to the sink, rinsed them out, and lined them up next to my Thermos.

I went upstairs and lay on my bed. I looked at the patterns the paint and patches made on the ceiling. It had been painted over plenty of times, and when I was little I used to see faces: goblins and witches and horrible animals, if I wanted to work myself up into a scare. I couldn't find the faces anymore. In my philosophical frame of mind I figured this was the price you paid for growing up.

There was a knock on the door and I dreaded it was Rosie, but what could I do, I had to let her in.

"Hi," Gary said, poking his head around the door. "You got time before dinner? I have news."

I practically jumped off the bed. "You found out?"

"Lotsa things, lotsa things," he said, sort of humming to himself. He walked in and slung his knapsack onto a chair. He walked around my room, staring at the pictures on the walls, at the books on the shelf, at my furniture. He even looked in my closet, cocking an eyebrow at me first as if to ask permission. I shrugged, feeling a little annoyed, but I figured it was necessary for the book, to get a feel for my personality or something.

When he was finished with the inspection, he came over to the bed and picked up the copy of *Thus Spake Zarathustra* that was still on my night table.

"You read Nietzsche?"

There was something in his voice. "Oh, sure," I said casually.

"Deep," Gary said.

"You going to put that in the book?"

"If it's important. Is it important?" He gave me a probing look.

I didn't know what to say. I promised myself I better read some Nietzsche just in case. I'd read it tonight. For now I better change the subject.

"Don't keep me in suspense, what did you find out?"

"You know that chick we rescued last night? I interviewed her."

"What the hell for?"

"She was so ungrateful, I wanted to get a thank-you. I didn't know you knew her."

"I don't know her."

"That's not what she says." He pulled the Velcro fasteners off his knapsack and took out a notebook. It was a small school notebook, the kind I used to take down homework assignments in. Gary flipped through the pages that were crammed with writing.

"She says, and I quote, 'Michael Thorn and I went to Jefferson Elementary together and to high school. We were in the same classes ever since fourth grade, when I moved to Kornkill from Chicago.' "

"She was in my class, that's all," I told Gary. "That doesn't mean I knew her."

"At least not in the biblical sense, right?" Gary asked, and winked.

"Not in any sense," I said.

He just grinned and closed the notebook and stuck it back in the knapsack.

"Hey, wait, what else did she say?"

"Sorry," Gary said. "I can't divulge a confidence."

"Oh, yeah? If it goes in your book, anybody can read it."

"I don't use everything people tell me," Gary said. "You've got to understand, it takes a lot of judgment."

When I didn't respond, he sat down on the edge of the bed. "Something the matter?"

"Nothing," I said.

"I did something wrong?" He punched at me.

"I was kidding. Here, you want to know what Mary Ann said about you?" He pulled the notebook out again and opened it up. "I quote: 'Michael Thorn is the biggest hunk in Kornkill. He's got bedroom eyes and he—'"

I grabbed for the book and Gary snatched it out of range.

"She didn't say anything like that."

"She didn't say anything bad, either, Mike," Gary said. "Trust me?"

I said okay. He told me Mary Ann worked in a hairdresser's on Main Street. Gary had gone downtown for lunch and passed the window and recognized her. Now he looked at his watch.

"Time to go up and slave over a hot plate," he said. "Tonight is ham and eggs à la Longman."

"What about the letters?" I said. "Did you find out?"

"I'm working on it," Gary said. "Come up later, we'll rap."

"Sure," I said as he hoisted the knapsack. The notebook was sticking out of the top. "So you don't have a tape recorder in your brain after all," I said.

"Huh?"

"Never mind."

"Later," he said, and closed the door.

Now I knew how Rosie felt. I wanted Gary to write the book but I didn't like the idea that he had things written down about me.

Mary Ann. What could she have said?

After Ginger McKee's funeral Mary Ann began

to talk to me at recess one day. She wore her hair in pigtails, she had great big front teeth, and the habit of picking at the skin around her fingernails. She told me about the funeral with gauzy eyes and she said, "It was something, Mickey," and I can still hear how she said it, it was *sumpin.* After that we used to stand around together at recess if we weren't on one of the game teams. Usually, I was never on a team because nobody picked me. Then summer came and I didn't see her and the next year I was in seventh grade and buddies with Wakefield and we didn't want to hang around with girls. Mary Ann drifted away.

Rosie called me for dinner. I went down. Rosie always made good lamb stew, but tonight I picked at it. Something was gnawing at me.

"Michael, eat your dinner," Rosie said.

"Don't waste good food," Grandpop intoned.

There had been something wrong with Gary's attitude when he came into my room tonight. He'd been excited at first, like he wanted to share something with me, and then he'd changed his mind, as if he realized he couldn't tell me. He was hiding something. That I didn't like.

I pushed the floury boiled potato across the river of gravy on my plate. How many times I'd dreamed of home cooking at the school, making lists of what I'd sacrifice: a tooth for a Skippy peanut butter sandwich, a toe for a pepperoni pizza. Now I could eat whatever I wanted and I didn't even care. The trouble with living the Perfectly Normal Life is that you don't realize how lucky you are. You grouse at all kinds of hardships: the Coke is warm, the potato chips are soggy, they didn't put enough pepperoni on the pizza.

"Michael! Are you eating or sleeping?" Rosie snapped.

I began to shovel the food in, reminding myself of the days of deprivation. I wished I could think of a way to talk to Mary Ann. There was something about Gary and her that bothered me. I had a bad feeling about it that wouldn't go away.

16

"Morning," Gary said, as I was pulling the storm windows out of the attic. He was in his undershorts and T-shirt and his beard looked scruffy. He scratched his hairy belly and looked at the windows. "Too hot for those, still summer outside."

"It won't last."

I expected him to ask why I hadn't come up to talk to him last night and I had an excuse ready. I'd been bugged last night, thinking about everything. I must have tossed around for hours, going from one gripe to another, sort of enjoying it, like biting on a canker sore. I had plenty of grievances. There was Lindsay calling me a paranoid fag, there was Gary taking his own sweet time to do me one lousy favor, there was Rosie giving me her sappy advice about hanging out with people my own age. Sure thing, Rosie, I would dig a few buddies up in the cemetery. Michael Thorn, resident pariah, was swamped with people his own age beating a path to his door. Who did I know who was my own age?

The answer just flowed effortlessly into my mind: Mary Ann. And suddenly I knew I had the solution to a problem and a way to take Rosie's advice, not that I wanted to do her any great favors.

If I wanted to talk to Mary Ann, maybe find out what she'd said to Gary that he was keeping such a big secret, I could do it easy. Ask her for a date. Rosie would be ecstatic.

But will Mary Ann be ecstatic? the smirking voice piped up—but I stomped on it and shut it up for once.

"Got a minute for a cup of coffee?" Gary asked. I could smell fresh-brewed coffee leaking out of the room behind him.

"Sure," I said. I had solved one problem and I was oozing confidence for solving another. "Smells good." And I followed him into his room.

There was a brand new electric coffeepot perking away on top of the bureau. So long to Rosie's veneer.

"You better hide that thing along with the toaster oven," I told him. He laughed. He found two mugs and poured the coffee. We sipped companionably for a few minutes. The room was a mess. You could hardly see the gateleg table under all his papers, and what you could see was covered with rings from Gary's coffee mugs. He drank coffee by the gallon when he was working, he had told me.

Gary must have been following my eyes. "I'll clean my room today!" he cried. "I promise to be good."

I had to chuckle. "Seriously, one of these days Rosie is going to kick you out."

"I don't think she comes up here anymore," he said. "One look was enough. No, it's not Rosie who is going to get rid of me, it's your grandfather."

That was a surprise. I hadn't even thought Grandpop bothered to acknowledge Gary's existence.

"I asked him a few questions," Gary explained. He waved his hand as if it had been burned. "Wooof. That man does not like to talk."

"But did he know *why* you wanted to talk to him?" It dawned on me that maybe Rosie had never bothered to explain Gary's presence to Grandpop.

"Oh, he knew why. He literally beat me off with a stick, like some mongrel dog."

My jaw must have dropped.

"Well, maybe that's an exaggeration," Gary amended. "He was taking his constitutional like he does every day after lunch and I decided to walk along with him. He suggested we take that path that goes up into the woods and I picked up a couple of fallen branches for us to use as walking sticks. We were rambling along with our shillelaghs, friendly as pie, until I started asking questions. He shook the stick in my face and told me where to get off."

The fact that Grandpop had been walking on the path that led to the cemetery bothered me more than his temper. Grandpop wouldn't put up with pushy questions, that was no surprise, although if it was going to help me in the end you'd think he'd make an exception. But forget that, I wondered how often Grandpop had walked on that path, and whether he'd ever been up to Murworth's Tomb.

"Don't look so worried, I'm not upset," Gary said. "Have some more joe."

"No thanks, I gotta go. I promised Rosie I'd do some chores."

"You're a good boy, Mike."

"Ha. That's what Rosie said. Listen, Gary, you know I asked you to check with the school about those letters?"

"Yeah, sure," he said lazily. "I told you, I'm working on it."

"What do you have to do to find out?"

That woke him up a little. "Well," he said. I could tell he hadn't been working on it at all. Bull-shit.

"Hey," he said. "What's happening here? We were getting along fine. Now all this distrust." He looked sheepish. "All right, all right, you caught me. I was so into other things, I put it off. Now you think I won't come through, don't you?"

I looked into my half-empty cup. "It's just that—"

"Not another word! I'll do it this morning. You'll have your answer tonight, how's that?" He stood up and saluted. He looked so goofy, with this belly hanging out over his shorts, I had to laugh. Some of my coffee spilled on Rosie's gray rug.

"Ah hah!" he cried. "Don't blame that one on me!"

He told me to get out, he had to get dressed, he had work to do.

I got the storm windows downstairs and told Rosie I'd put them in even if it was warm. You never knew, it might turn cold overnight.

"You're feeling chipper this morning," Rosie said.

The truth was I was feeling a little shitty for doubting Gary. Maybe I was living in the past, still screwed up by the school. You had to be suspicious to survive there, you couldn't trust anybody—not only the kids, the staff as well. You could get written up for anything—maybe they didn't like the color of your tie—and you'd find yourself in solitary, or taking the bench, or doing the yard.

"Aren't you going up to work today?" Rosie asked, coming out to perch on the porch rail as I worked on the kitchen door.

"Yep. Linny doesn't mind if I take some time off. He's having a lull right now. Death is taking a vacation."

The air was light and fresh and I felt pretty good. Deep in my stomach a roller coaster was doing dips about asking Mary Ann for a date, but I had it under control. I looked up to smile at Rosie and saw she was wearing her unhappy face.

"What's the matter?"

"I told Pop what you said about interviews for the book. It seems Mr. Longman already spoke to him about it. Pop put him straight. Now I'm thinking that Mr. Longman's staying here isn't such a good idea."

"No, Rosie!" I cried without thinking. "I mean, you can't tell him that. Does Grandpop say he has to leave?"

"Not quite." Rosie's eyes were searching my face. "Does it mean so much to you that he stays?"

I felt my face flush. Did it? It must, because there was a churning in my gut that had nothing to do with a date with Mary Ann.

"Yes," I managed to say. Rosie looked away from me, trying to hide her suddenly tearful eyes.

"Oh, Michael," she said, lifting her hands and letting them fall back into her lap. She brushed at her eyes and sniffed. "Let's not worry about it. We'll leave it as it is for now." She patted my arm and went inside.

I finished changing the screens to the windows, feeling shaky, like me and my future had had a close call. I jumped when Gary's voice said, "Need a ride?"

He was all decked out in a shirt and tie, V-necked sweater, tweed jacket, and cords. And his white sneakers.

"I'm going to the cemetery," I said.

"Come on, I'll drop you off." He tossed me his car keys. "You can drive." I leaned the screens up against the house and put the screwdriver back. I yelled to Rosie that I was leaving.

"Your lunch!" I heard her say from somewhere

in the house. I grabbed the paper bag from the counter and stuck the Thermos under my arm.

I drove us to the cemetery, not too shabby, if I do say so myself. No stalls, nice turns, easy on the gears. Gary said, "Great going," as he slid over to the driver's side when I got out.

"I'm gonna get you your facts," he said.

"Yeah, I believe you."

He turned the car around and headed out of the gates. I waited for a couple of minutes. Then I stashed my lunch in the workshed and went to find Linny. I told him I'd be back in a while. "Not to worry," he said in his mild way. "The job can wait another hour."

It was dumb, but I didn't know the name of the place where Mary Ann worked, so I couldn't make a call. And I hadn't wanted Gary to even drop me off in town instead of the cemetery. He'd right away start asking questions. So I prepared to slog back downtown. Maybe I could catch a bus on Monrovia Boulevard. What I needed was wheels.

I felt like a criminal in a way. What if I bumped into Gary again?

I wondered where he had been going, all dressed up. Usually he wore blue jeans and a sweat shirt. His "artist's habit," Rosie called it, making a pun.

I was jogging along when I heard a car horn beep. I stopped in my tracks, afraid to look around and see Gary's car.

"Mickey, where are you going?" Rosie said, leaning out of Moira's rusty Chevrolet.

"Town. Doing an errand for Linny," I lied.

"Hop in," Moira said in her gravelly voice. She had her usual cigarette stuck between her lips. She never took it out when she talked.

I climbed into the backseat, like an obedient dog.

"We're slumming," Moira told me, stepping on the gas so that the car jerked forward. "We're going to try all the new shops downtown."

Rosie looked a little nervous at this prospect, but Moira's big freckled face was aglow.

"Linny shouldn't be sending you all the way to town," Rosie said primly. "Your job isn't to be an errand boy."

Moira cackled. "You're looking very healthy, Mickey. Civilian life agrees with you." Rosie gasped.

"I really think I should speak to Heva," she said.

"He's a big boy now," said Moira. She winked at me in the mirror.

"Don't say anything to anybody," I cried from the backseat. Both of them looked startled.

Oh, what the hell, I thought. "It's a personal errand," I confessed.

Moira's eyes began to twinkle. "Is it a gal?" she blurted. Rosie looked concerned.

"I'm not telling," I said, trying to sound light-hearted.

"Where do you want us to drop you off?" Rosie

asked, and I could see she was struggling between apprehension and relief.

"This corner will be fine," I said, not having a clue where Mary Ann worked.

"Don't worry," I said to Rosie as I crawled out of the car. "It's someone my own age."

Rosie looked blank for a moment and then her face blossomed like a flower.

At least someone's happy, I thought, as Moira sputtered off in a cloud of fumes. I looked around furtively, in case Gary was lurking. Then I started down the street, keeping an eye peeled for hairdressers.

I passed a barber shop, obviously wrong. In the next block there was a promising sign: Carousel Coiffures. I made a Pink Panther–type reconnaissance of the area and then slipped into the doorway of the shop. I'd planned to have a discreet peek in the window, to see if I spotted Mary Ann. That's what Gary said he'd done—seen her as he was passing by. Only thing, as I gave a peek, somebody opened the door of the shop and walked into me. In the middle of the excuse-me's and such, I looked up and saw everybody looking at the door. There was Mary Ann all right, with her eyes popping, and in one hand she had scissors poised and in the other hand she held up a long brown strand of hair that belonged to none other than Iraleen Johnson, Lindsay's mother.

17

It was probably the best thing that could have happened, because it broke the ice.

I raced out of that doorway and caught a bus going up to Monrovia Boulevard. When I got back to the cemetery, I wolfed down my lunch and then got instructions from Linny. The moratorium on death was over. Old Dr. Garber, the town dentist for at least a hundred years, had died in the early morning. He would be going into the ground in a few days. Linny thought it was a good idea to dig now, while it was so warm. So I got started measuring out the plot, keeping an eye on the time. And then before I actually began to break ground, I went out to the boulevard, found a pay phone, and put in a call to Carousel Coiffures. I figured by this time Iraleen's hair would be done and she would be gone.

"Mickey!" Mary Ann said when she heard who it was. "What was that all about before?" she demanded, but she didn't sound mad. Maybe I was imagining it, but she might have sounded glad to hear from me.

"I'll explain," I said. "Could I see you tonight?" It was easy. And just as easy, she said yes. Only then I remembered the problem of no wheels and felt embarrassed.

"I'll pick you up," she said. Just like that. I didn't even have to explain. We agreed on eight o'clock.

"Bye for now, Mickey," she said in her sweet, frail voice. It tingled in my ear all the way back to work.

I started up the backhoe and began chopping earth. Like the holes he used to drill in people's teeth, I'd made Dr. Garber a nice neat excavation. And then Dr. Garber himself could be the filling.

I worked steadily, almost hypnotized by the droning rise and fall of the motor, until I thought I might be digging old Garber's hole too deep. I killed the hoe and got out. It was hot. I took off my shirt and wiped the sweat off my face.

"Yooo hooo, Michael," I heard Aunt Heva call from her porch. I gave her a wave. "Can I bring you a cold drink?" I called back, "Yeah," and she disappeared into the house.

I went over to have a look at the hole. It was sort of melancholy, standing on the edge of Garber's eternity, looking down and knowing I was going to end up like that myself one day. Most of the time I didn't get morbid about death when I worked. Like Linny, I was used to it. I guess it was just my present philosophical state of mind.

I was aware of something moving toward me at

the far corner of my eye. Aunt Heva coming with the drink. I sure could use it.

I mopped my head again with my rolled-up shirt. I could almost feel that cold liquid running down my throat. What would I give for a cold drink if I were back at the school? Not a tooth, not worth it, because I could take a swig from the fountain as soon as I went back to the hall. Maybe it was worth a fingernail. Or eyelashes. Gosh, I remember Lindsay used to say she liked my eyelashes.

The pain was neat and contained. It moved efficiently down the side of my neck, into my shoulder, along my arm. I thought: that's a masterpiece, who taught it to move quite like that?

Like a long blinding whip of heat, a sunshine pain, appropriate for an Indian summer day. Yet it was also cool and swift, it went to the quick and pierced me so brilliantly that I was disappointed when it ended with such a dull and mundane ache.

I felt myself going, slipping over the edge of the world, and I floated down down into the grave of night, thought to myself: Boy, it's dark in here, Garber's going to need a flashlight. I began to laugh, but stopped when the thud came. The earth came up and smacked me flat and then I just lay there and thought it would be nice to go to sleep, but something in the back of my bruised mind told me it wasn't nice to fall asleep in somebody else's grave.

I think I had a long dream. People were dancing. I told this guy to stop bugging me or I would let him have it. Freegull was there, shaking me awake. Hey, you dummy, can't you hear the bell? The air smelled like the ammonia of fear.

"Michael, can you hear me?"

I opened my eyes against something soft and cottony. Aunt Heva's chest. The sky spun around, made me dizzy. I felt like throwing up.

"Awwaw," I told her but that didn't sound right. For God's sake, was I going to have another speech impediment? I couldn't stand it if they sent me back. But they wouldn't do that for a little relapse.

"Just a lidda welap," I said.

"Oh, my stars, take it easy," Aunt Heva said.

I tried only one eye this time. Not too bad. Aunt Heva was helping me to sit up. We were both of us down at the bottom of the mudhole I'd dug.

"What happened?"

"I don't know, Mickey," she said, her chest heaving, voice fluttering. "I came out with the soda and you weren't anywhere. I saw the hoe, I came over to look for you, and there you were, lying down here. I had a shock! My heart can't take it, seeing you lying at the bottom of an open grave. Before I gave it a thought, I jumped in. A foolish thing for an old woman to do. Mickey, I don't think I'm going to be able to climb back out." She stopped to take a breath. I hung my head between my knees to stop the spinning.

"Are you all right now? You must have lost your balance."

"Somebody hit me."

"Too muddy, you need to be careful. This weather is a sin. It's unnatural. You just slipped on the edge."

"Somebody hit me on the head." I tried to stand up. The walls of the pit looked insurmountable. "Where's Linny?"

"Why, I don't know. I think he's around somewhere. We'll give him a call."

"Oh, Christ." I tried to get a foothold in the crumbly damp earth. I kicked at the wall with my shoe to make a notch.

"Michael be careful, you might be hurt."

"Damn right I'm hurt." I could feel something growing like a melon on the back of my head.

Viciously, I kicked out another notch and pushed my shoe in. I grabbed at the pale, spooky tendrils of underground roots. I used to hate them, they were so tough, they'd clog the hoe. Now I was glad to see the buggers. I hoisted myself up to the grass, my legs flailing like a fish.

Linny was coming across from the woods and I wouldn't have blamed him for dropping dead of fright. I must have looked like something, dragging myself out of a grave.

He came running. "What happened? You fall in?"

"Help Aunt Heva," I said and walked around the side of the hoe and lost my lunch.

I heard Aunt Heva groaning and Linny grunting and the earth crumbling like a waterfall. I wiped

my mouth with the back of my hand and went to
help. We managed to haul her out. She collapsed in
a heap and Linny sat down beside her, panting and
sweating himself.

"He says somebody pushed him," Aunt Heva
gasped.

Several yards away I saw something glinting in
the grass. I went toward it and it winked at me. The
glass that had held the soda, empty now, lying
where Aunt Heva had dropped it. I turned and
looked back at the fresh grave. Linny had his arm
around his wife, comforting her. There was no way
you could see the bottom of the grave from here.

"Did you see anyone, Aunt Heva?" I asked,
coming back.

She put her hand to her throat and looked up in
a worried, frightened, or maybe it was a secretive
way. "I didn't see a soul," she said in barely a
whisper.

"Let's get you back to the house, Heva," said
Linny. "And we must call an ambulance for Michael,
he's bleeding."

"I'll just go home," I said. I felt foggy, but I
could make it. No ambulance. No police.

It was a funny thing: Aunt Heva said so quickly,
"You drive him Linny, so there's no fuss."

Rosie screamed when she saw Linny helping
me out of his funereal black car. Grandpop came
downstairs to see what was going on. Linny explained I'd fallen and hit my head. I didn't contra-
dict him.

"The doctor," Rosie said, going for the phone. I said I didn't need the doctor and Grandpop backed me up, probably because of the cost.

"He'll live," he said, inspecting my head. "It just needs to be cleaned up."

Rosie sat me down at the kitchen table and put a towel around my shoulders. She mopped away the blood and mud and poured peroxide over the wound. It stung.

"At least there's a lump, that's a good sign. They say when you hit your head you should get a lump. Otherwise, the injury goes inside the brain."

"Terrific," I said.

She made me close my eyes and touch my nose with a finger, she made me walk a straight line down the hall runner, and I had to follow her finger as it moved back and forth in front of my face.

"We have to look out for concussion," she said, spilling the basin of dirty reddish water into the sink.

"I'll go lie down for a while."

"No!" Rosie cried. "Don't go to sleep. You might fall into a coma."

"Okay, Doc," I said. "Where'd you learn all this stuff?"

"From books, where else?" Rosie said, and I wondered if she had switched to reading medical romances.

I sat on the edge of my bed, sipping the hot tea with lemon that Rosie insisted I have as a stimulant to keep me awake.

I closed my eyes anyway, but not to sleep. I played the tape over in my brain, trying to remember everything. Standing near the hole, wiping my face with my shirt. Thinking that I saw Aunt Heva out of the corner of my eye. Coming toward me with a cool drink. Blip. Replay. Aunt Heva coming toward me. Replay. *Someone* coming toward me. Hold. I stared at the picture, but it was too fuzzy. Every time I thought something was taking shape, the picture blurred and I was left with only the vague teasing outline of a human shape.

Aunt Heva hadn't hit me on the head. But she most certainly saw who did. Because she dropped the glass too soon. What did she tell me? "I looked and you weren't around. I came over and saw you lying at the bottom of the grave." That glass should have been dropped right on the edge of the hole, not nine or ten yards away. The question was, who was Aunt Heva shielding?

I must have drifted off to sleep anyway, in spite of Rosie's warnings. But I didn't fall into a coma. Gary woke me and for a moment I was disoriented and afraid, feeling his hand on my shoulder, shaking me.

He looked relieved as I opened my eyes. "You okay? Rosie said she called upstairs and didn't get an answer."

"I'm fine." I had a hell of a headache, but I figured that was par for the course.

"I heard you had an accident."

"Stupid mistake. I fell into a grave."

"You *fell* into a grave?" Gary said, looking incredulous, his mouth twitching as if he wasn't sure he should laugh.

"Must be some black humor in that," I said, and smiled. Then winced. Who would think a smile could go all the way around to the back of your head?

Gary guffawed. "That's a good one. I'll have to put that in a book. Listen, kid, I got some news. Maybe good, maybe bad, depends on what you hoped the answer would be. I can tell you with all certainty that the school never kept any letters from getting to you. In fact, the guy that takes care of the mail, what's his name? Duffy? He remembered you getting letters and he said he always put them in your box. The school has no policy for censoring mail and it's hard enough to get an order when they need one, like if a kid might be planning an escape. Duffy said he never got any orders on you."

I looked at Gary's fancy outfit. "What'd you do, go up to the school?"

"No, no. I called them."

"You talked to Duffy?"

"Sure. Listen, never mind my methods, they're full of madness, ha ha. You sure you feel all right?"

"Sure."

"Sure?" He looked so genuinely concerned.

"Naw, I feel lousy. It was bad news, what you said about the letters."

"Your girl friend's lying?"

"She's not my girl friend anymore. But yes, I

guess she was lying. It makes me feel bad, that she would have to put on such an act. I don't know."

"Maybe the letters just got lost."

"A couple maybe, but not a whole year's worth."

"So you don't think she's lying? You think she really sent the letters?"

"It seems a stupid thing to lie about. She could have made a bunch of excuses I probably would have believed."

Gary frowned. "I wish I knew more about this girl."

"Her name's Lindsay Johnson. She lives a few streets over. She was my only best friend since I was a kid. Now her mother won't even let me speak to her."

"Because you were sent away?"

"She's scared of me! She thinks I'm a murderer. Everybody thinks so."

"And you didn't commit any murder," Gary mumbled to himself.

"Hey, what is this? I thought you were on my side. Don't you start, too!" I tried to get up, I think I would have socked him, but a wave of nausea slapped me back down on the bed.

"Sorry, Mike, I think you misunderstood. It's just my way, getting the facts straight in my mind. No, I think we should look into this business about the letters."

I wasn't really sure I cared anymore whether Lindsay was lying to me or not. But the thing nagged at me. It was another one of those uncertainties, a loose end that maybe I needed to tie up before I could get this whole business out of my life.

"If the letters really did exist, I don't know how you're going to find out what happened," I said. "What can you do, march into the Kornkill post office and ask them?"

"Not a bad idea," Gary said.

"Oh, come on. She could put them in any mailbox."

"Somebody might remember. What I've learned is that if you ask enough questions, you very often get answers." Gary pulled over the chair from my desk. "First, do we have any corroborating evidence that there were letters? Aside from Lindsay's word for it, that is."

"You sound like a lawyer. As a matter of fact, we do. Aunt Heva, that's Mrs. Pollard up at the cemetery, says Lin wrote me all the time. And Rosie says so, too. But, you can't really believe them. They might have just assumed Lin was writing me, you know, because they expected her to."

"Sure," Gary broke in, "but we can ask if they actually saw the letters, or envelopes addressed to you."

Oh, boy, Rosie would love being interrogated.

"I guess," I said. "But just don't ask my grandfather anything about it."

"I think we have something interesting here," Gary said. He leaped up from the chair. "I'm very curious about this. You get some rest, your head looks like *Star Wars*. I'll see you later."

"There's only one thing, Gary," I said, and he paused with his hand on the doorknob. "How do letters fit in? How can they have anything to do with that night in the park?" I couldn't see how solving the mystery of some letters could relate to the murder.

"There's only one thing I know for sure," Gary said, "and that's that nothing is."

I gave him a sick smile. I wanted to ask if he'd bring me two aspirin, but he was already out the door and I didn't have the strength to call him back. Maybe I was falling into the dreaded coma. I closed my eyes.

"And listen, Mike," I heard Gary say as he came into the room again. "Not everybody thinks you're Jack the Ripper."

"Michael the Murderer," I corrected.

"You ought to know that some people are for you."

"Thanks." I meant it. I almost felt like crying when he shut the door, but maybe that was because my head was hurting so bad.

After a few minutes, as I was slipping into a kind of fitful sleep, I wanted to call after him: "Hey, wait a minute. I didn't tell you the whole truth and nothing but the truth about this afternoon."

Keep your head, kid, the voice inside me said. Yeah, that's right.

The reason I hadn't mentioned it was because it

seemed to me just a repeat of the night in Monrovia Park. Michael sees a woman get pushed off the wall. Nobody believes him. Michael gets hit on the head in the cemetery. Nobody believes him. In both cases eyewitnesses tell a different story.

Come to think of it, I should ask Gary to find out who that previous eyewitness had been. It would be interesting to see if Gary could really perform miracles.

18

I didn't forget my date with Mary Ann, but it sure was hard getting myself out of my stupor to take a shower. And then it was even harder to convince Rosie I could go.

I think the only reason she relented was because she had been so happy to see me acting rehabilitated. If I had a date with a girl who used to be in my class, then things couldn't be so bad, could they?

If you're ever nervous about a date, I highly recommend you get bashed on the head beforehand. Because then you won't get cold feet, you'll be too busy begging for mercy from the shower beating on your wounds and you'll be too busy trying not to throw up to worry about your nerves.

I got dressed in slow motion and went down for dinner. On the way out of my room I smelled cooking from the third floor—Gary must have been frying sausages—and I almost gagged. When I looked down at my plate of reheated lamb stew and coleslaw, I almost fainted.

"I need a Coke," I said, and went to the kitchen. When I came back, Grandpop said, "Eat only if you feel like it, Michael." Rosie looked tight-lipped, so I knew they must have had words about it. I threw Grandpop a grateful glance and shoved the plate away.

Mary Ann honked at eight o'clock sharp and I ran out, hoping Rosie wouldn't stand at the door waving forlornly, but she did, of course.

"God, what happened to you?" Mary Ann asked when she saw my bandaged head. "I was going to suggest we try Patrick's Pub, but you look like you need someplace quiet."

"Quiet would be nice," I said. "Sorry to ruin the plans. But get going wherever it is before Rosie comes out to remind us to be good."

Mary Ann laughed. "I've got one of those at home myself," she said, and waved at Rosie. Immediately, the front door shut.

"Touché," said Mary Ann, and we took off down Carhart Street.

"So, you gonna tell me what happened?"

I debated precisely three seconds, and then I told her. "Somebody tried to kill me."

I expected a big laugh, but Mary Ann said, "You mean it?"

"Well, it wasn't a love tap." I explained what had happened.

"Who would do a thing like that?"

"That's what I'd like to know. And the funny thing is, I think I do know." I told her how I'd seen the person coming toward me. "But the trouble is, I was expecting it to be Aunt Heva, and so I sort of superimposed her on whoever it really was. I have this feeling that the moment I was hit, I realized who it was. But when I came to, the memory was gone."

"Like amnesia."

"I guess so. Except I remember everything else."

Mary Ann skillfully pulled out onto the parkway. This afternoon I'd been thinking of suggesting I drive and worrying if she'd let me, or if I'd do all right. My head had solved the problem.

"Maybe you're repressing it," she said. "Like you don't want to know."

I must have looked surprised, because she added, tartly, "What's wrong, don't you think a hairstylist can have a brain?"

"You've got it wrong. That was relief. I've had psychiatrists coming out of my ears so long, I began to think like them. And I didn't expect anybody else to understand. You'll have to make allowances," I joked. "I've been living a sheltered life."

Mary Ann smiled. Her front teeth didn't look too big anymore; I guess her face had grown to fit.

"It's not your fault anyway," she said. "I'm just touchy. Do you know practically everybody in our class went away to college? They made a big thing about it at graduation. For the first time in the history of Kornkill High School, we have ninety-stupid percent of our graduates going on to blah blah blah. Ten kids in the big Ivy League."

"Yeah, Wakefield went to Dartmouth, I think."

"Williams. I felt so mad, they made me feel like I was deprived or just plain stupid. At the prom people would say, 'Oh, where are you going, Mary Ann?' And if I said nowhere, they gave me this pitying look, and if I mentioned the beauty institute, they got all patronizing. 'Oh, that'll be nice, won't it, you can do my hair!' "

"That's bad," I said.

"Really. If they ever come in to get their hair done, I think I'll do something terrible!" She laughed. Her laughter was like her voice, you had to hold on to it before it got away. I wanted to hold on to it.

We went into a new place off the parkway, where they had espresso coffee and pastries. "This used to be that greasy-spoon diner, remember?" Mary Ann said.

We found a table in the back. Soft music was coming out of some speakers in the ceiling. The lighting was soft and muted. Every table had a candle flickering. It smelled of coffee and spice.

"This is nice," I told her.

"All summer this was the in spot for the big-deal college crowd. They think they discovered something. Little do they know my mother's brother-in-law put up some of the money for this place."

"Hey, it doesn't matter," I told her, and she looked questioning at me. "It doesn't matter what they think. Be your own person."

She looked down at her hands, and then the waitress brought the menu and we ordered cappuccino and cheesecake.

"You ever think of that picnic?" she asked me when the waitress went away.

I was jolted. "Yes. I do."

"I didn't. Not until that reporter started asking me questions about the past. Then I remembered, and after he left, you know what I did? I went into the john and cried."

She fumbled with her napkin, as if she might cry now. "Isn't that silly? After all this time?"

"Not silly," I said. I took her hand and she held on and we stayed that way, even when the coffee and pastry came. And I realized I'd almost forgotten why I had wanted to ask her out. Whatever she'd said to Gary, I didn't care, I didn't even want to talk about it now.

Instead, we talked about the school, about Freegull and Kline. Our coffee got cold.

"Maybe I shouldn't say it, but Mrs. Johnson is really hung up about you," she said when we let go hands to eat our cheesecake.

"I'd like to know why."

She paused, a forkful of cheesecake on the way to her mouth. "You were dating Lindsay before you left, right? She doesn't want you to start again. It's just being narrow minded."

"She's awfully hyper about it."

Mary Ann looked at me. "Do you plan to date Lindsay again?" she asked, and then bit her lip. "God, that was a giveaway!"

"It's all over with Lindsay," I told her.

"That's really your business," she said. "I shouldn't have asked."

"It *is* over. I think Lindsay knows it, too. Now, if she'd just explain that to her mother, Iraleen could stop worrying and cancel her shrink."

"But maybe Lindsay doesn't want it to be over," Mary Ann said. And I thought of Lin's hurt eyes and knew Mary Ann was right.

We ate in silence for a while. The atmosphere was soothing and I was having unexpectedly very nice feelings about Mary Ann. I was enjoying myself except for the intermittent throbbing of my skull.

"You all right?" Mary Ann asked.

"I think so."

"You look pale. Maybe I should take you home."

"I'm some date, huh?"

Mary Ann looked very serious. "It was wonderful."

"Yeah, it was." I got the check. I helped Mary Ann on with her coat and we went out to the car. She started to laugh as she got in behind the wheel. "I was just thinking about this morning. I thought you were coming in for a haircut, but you just disappeared."

"I didn't know how to phone you. Gary told me you worked on Main Street."

"Gary, the reporter. How come you know him?"

"Didn't he tell you? He's writing a book about me."

Mary Ann seemed puzzled. "He just said he was doing a follow-up on a bunch of unsolved murders and Monrovia Park was one of them. I don't even know why he wanted to talk to me."

"He's crazy over grass roots."

Mary Ann giggled and I reached out and touched her hair. It was smooth and soft, falling in waves around her shoulders. She leaned against me and I put my arms around her. I didn't want to but I had to ask her.

"Do you think I had anything to do with Monrovia Park?"

She sat up and turned the key in the ignition. "Of course not. I never did. It was all trumped up. At the time it made me mad, but I was a kid and nobody wanted to hear my opinion." The engine roared and we swung out of the parking lot.

I wished I'd known then she was in my corner. But it didn't hurt to know now. "What made you so sure?"

She kept her eyes on the road as she ticked off her reasons, rapping a finger on the steering wheel with each one.

"One, you had a date with Lindsay that night. I knew because she made a big thing about it in the girls' locker room and I overheard and thought she was acting like a silly kid. Two, everybody knew you were crazy about Lindsay, so there wasn't any reason for you to be meeting another girl in the park that same night. Three, Lindsay's own father said you walked into the park, went straight to the bottom of the wall, saw something, and ran out. So how could you have been the one who pushed the girl off?"

"What did you say?"

"I said how could you have been—"

"No, before that. Lindsay's *father* saw me?" Boyd Johnson was the eyewitness. It hit me like a ton of bricks, took the wind out of my lungs, and made my head ring like a cannon.

"Michael, you want me to stop the car?" Mary Ann asked in alarm.

"No, I'm all right. Give me a minute. Can you tell me why Lindsay's father was in the park that night?"

"I think I just made a boo-boo," Mary Ann said. "Back then he wanted to keep it a secret, I guess. He'd been spying on you and Lin for ages because he didn't like you dating her, being only fourteen. He hung out at the park, waiting to catch you doing something you shouldn't, I guess."

"Cripes. How do you know all this?"

"Iraleen Johnson."

I must have looked at her like she was nuts. "She confided in you?"

"My mother owns the Carousel. I always went there after school to help out and do shampoos. I heard Mrs. Johnson talking all the time, my mom used to do her hair. She was always down on you but never like she is now."

"It must have galled her when her own husband gave me an alibi."

Mary Ann considered. "No, she seemed very fair about that. I sort of admired her for it, I'm ashamed to say."

It was a lot to take in all at once. I felt dizzy again. Mary Ann drove me straight to No. 5 Carhart Street. If I'd been my more usual self, I would have been annoyed. I had this great desire to put my arms around Mary Ann again, to kiss her. But I can't say I was sorry to see home.

"Thanks," I said. "I'm sorry I'm in such bad shape."

Mary Ann leaned forward and her lips touched my lips.

"I hope I see you again, Michael," she said softly, and her voice was like the scent of a flower you can't quite capture.

"Me, too."

She held my hand tightly in hers. "If you can, I think you should try to remember about this afternoon."

"I wish I could," I said. "I'll try."

I watched the car turn at the end of the street, the red blip of the blinker fading out of sight. As I walked to the house, I shivered. The weather had turned.

Rosie must have been standing right inside the door, because she pounced on me the minute I came in. She wanted to know all about my date.

"It was a nice date," I told her. "It was a very proper date. It was a date that might lead to more dates. I'm going to bed now."

"Michael! Are you feeling all right? You seem queer."

"Funny thing, that's what Lindsay said." I put my foot on the stairs. I wondered if I could make it to the top. "It's getting cold outside, Rosie. Winter is here."

19

I'm in Gary's room and he's talking to me in a steady, monotonous voice. He's suggesting I go to sleep. In a few moments I'll be hypnotized. And then we'll find out who tried to kill me.

It was his idea, and although I don't have much faith in hypnotism, I'm patiently waiting for it to take effect. He's been hypnotized himself and assures me there's no danger. In a trance I might be able to replay those moments in the cemetery and remember who it was I saw out of the corner of my eye.

"You're getting drowsy. . . ." Gary says. I think he sounds like Boris Karloff in some horror flick. I think I should say, "Let's forget it," but my body stays in the chair, like a hunk of lead.

I had told Gary about the cemetery. After all that stuff about Lindsay's parents, I felt I needed advice. And just like Mary Ann, he said I was probably blocking the identity of the person I saw come up behind me in the cemetery. Like I was afraid to know.

And now he's telling me I feel drowsy. And then I'm getting a funny feeling that's more like a sound and I feel as if something is pushing me. I feel a little scared at first, and it hurts my head.

But it's all right, I'm not in any danger. I'm sitting in some kind of contraption, being pushed forward, and I'm familiar with this feeling. There's a long avenue lined with trees and a church with a tall spire. And here is Rosie coming toward us, wearing a flowered dress, walking in high-heeled shoes, her legs thin and shiny. She bends down and looks me in the eye. I remember that I like Rosie. We come here to wait for her, by the church. Behind me my mother's voice is talking.

Now I'm sitting in a shady hall and smelling flowers that grow on the vines near the door. A woman comes down the hall, I hear her coming and her shadow falls across the porch, growing bigger and bigger until I'm afraid to see a monster appear, but when I look up I see my mother. She leans down to me, lifts me up, and I sail into the sky. She's laughing.

My mother's arms are around me, telling me a story about the moon. She points to colors in a book she holds, but I am not looking at the pictures. I look into my mother's face and see the mystery of her eyes, as blue as two moons in a white sea, and her hair flowing long around her shoulders, tickling my ears as she holds me close. I smell my mother's smell, the nighttime waking-up scent of solace and the morning sun of lemon, and the day stretches out and I don't know whether it's a year or a hundred or when I have been born or when the night will come again.

Grandfather comes wearing a shiny watch across his stomach, carrying two shopping bags of food. My mother is crying. My grandfather is talking, in the voice like a rumbling thunderstorm. I push my head under my blanket and the voice follows me and I squeeze my eyes shut and finally there is the thunderboom and my grandfather is gone.

My mother touches me, but I don't move. I pretend I'm sleeping and she goes away. I hear her soft footsteps disappearing into the long dark night. And after that there is only Rosie.

Someone is calling me. I want to sleep. I'll stay here and sleep and never wake up. It must be time for school, I overslept again. Rosie will be mad. The alarm clock never works, or else I slam it when it rings and go back to sleep again. I haven't studied for the math quiz.

The bell is ringing now and Freegull is going to start shaking my shoulder.

"Michael. Wake up!"

Why don't they go away? The layers are disappearing so fast, I can't see the bottom anymore. I'm rising upward, in fact I can fly. It's easy, I don't know why I never thought of it before.

"Michael!"

"What do you want?"

"Thank God." It's Gary. He's white as a sheet. Drops of perspiration are sticking out all over his face like he's just come out of the shower. He asks,

"You all right? You awake?" Then he slumps into a chair and covers his face with his hands.

"Hey, what's wrong?" I ask him. "Didn't I remember who it was?"

He doesn't say anything at all.

"Hey, Gary? What's up?"

"I should have known better," he mumbles into his hands. He looks at me. "I'm sorry I put you through all that."

I shrug. "What's the big deal? Did I say something weird?"

"You don't remember?"

I shake my head. "Had some dreams." I laugh. "Dreamed I was flying. Look, are you gonna tell me what's wrong?"

"You talked about your mother."

"I did? Did I say something bad?"

"No, no. It was"—he licks his lips—"it was just an emotional experience, that's all. Nobody has a right to pry into the most private parts of another person's mind."

"Don't feel bad. Did I cry or something? I don't really feel emotional about it anymore. My mother died a long time ago. I'm used to it now. You know? I hardly think about it anymore."

"No," Gary says, looking more ashen.

"I'm telling you, man, don't worry."

"Your mother's not dead. She's alive."

His words rolled toward me, like a garble. I wasn't sure I heard.

"What? What're you, crazy?"

Suddenly he jumps out of his chair and comes and kneels down in front of me. Kneels down. It makes me feel uncomfortable, sort of creepy. He takes my hands. I snatch them back. "Come on, Gary." I think the guy has gone wonco.

"Michael, I don't know what you've been told and maybe I have no right to say this, but your mother is alive, not dead."

"Right now?"

He nods.

"Where? Where is she?"

Part of me is galloping through some time warp, trying to catch up to my guts, which are flying all over my brain.

"I don't know. That's the truth. She was in Amber Knoll for a long time but she's not there anymore."

"Amber Knoll is a mental hospital."

Gary nods again.

I get up from the chair. He's still on the floor and I feel like kicking him in the teeth. I feel like breaking his stinking neck.

"I thought you were my friend. I told you everything and you have all kinds of secrets you don't tell me. What else do you know? Got any more surprises up your sleeve?"

"Calm down," Gary says, getting to his feet. "I'm sorry. I thought I was doing the right thing. I don't like to interfere with people's lives."

"What a crock! You're interfering just by being in this house. And what about when your book comes out? What a great way for me to find out about my mother. Were you going to put that in? Michael Thorn's mother was a nut case? And what about my grandfather? He's an old man. The shock could kill him."

Gary looks tired out. "Who do you think paid all her medical bills?" he says.

"You shit!"

Gary makes those waving motions with his hands that he always does when he's playing for time.

"Maybe you're right," he says. "I was fooling myself. I got more involved than I counted on. Take it easy, okay? I don't have any more secrets. I swear, no more skeletons in the closet." He puts his hands up in surrender. "I'm clean, see?"

"All right, it's not your fault," I say, turning away so I can get rid of the tears that are running down my face. "I understand."

Inside of me the pieces that were flying around are slowing down, like a big merry-go-round grinding to a halt. Small slivers of my heart clink back into place.

"It's not your fault, but I'd like to know what kind of game Grandpop and Rosie thought they were playing."

"Maybe they thought it was for your own good."

"Bunch of hypocrites."

"Don't judge them too harshly."

"Oh, shut up, you sound like a soap opera. I have a right to be angry."

"You do, that's for sure."

"I have to go now. I have to think about all this. Don't say anything to them, okay?"

"Of course not," Gary says very quietly.

"And you're my friend, right? You can help me get this straight?"

"I'll do whatever I can."

I go out into the hall. Downstairs, I hear Rosie humming. She says something to my grandfather and he rumbles an answer back. Dirty bastards, I think. I wait until the coast is clear and go to my room and lock myself in.

20

It bothers me, it bothers me. How many times have I been suckered? Why didn't I remember the lessons I learned at the school? I'm a bigger jerk than Andrew Bartlett III, I deserve everything I got. Freegull would sneer at me. Freegull would never have let this happen to him.

God, if my mother was crazy, maybe I am, too. Is craziness an inheritable thing? Maybe all this stuff about Monrovia Park is just in my head. I *could* have killed that girl. Look at what I did after, walking into people's houses, saying I was looking for answers. Answers to what? Once insane, always insane. It runs in the family. My grandfather is probably crazy, too. That's why he didn't tell me about my mother.

Long ago, she died long ago, he'd said. Far away. Better not talk about it. But Rosie, she should have told the truth. She says lying is a sin. Isn't it a sin to lie about the death of one's mother? That must be a mortal sin if there ever was one.

Now Gary. Are you my friend, Gary? Sure, sure, he says. But what's in it for him? I've got to make sure. If I don't, I'll go crazy. Ha ha, that's a laugh. How can you go crazy when you're already crazy?

I've got to find out. He says he doesn't know where my mother is, but that could be a lie. Rosie and Grandpop told me lies for my own good, maybe Gary feels the same way. He doesn't want me to find my mother. He could be playing a trick on me.

Give the guy a break. He's been a buddy. Teaching me how to drive. He's been pretty straight. I can understand how he didn't want to say anything, I really can. Maybe Grandpop threatened him. Did it for my own good. Poor guy. Wanted to spare me. Give the guy a chance.

But I gotta check. I gotta know.

My mind was going a million miles an hour. I couldn't stop it. Rosie came up and knocked on my door. "Everything all right, Mickey?"

"Everything's peachy keen," I told her.

"Well"—she hesitated—"then I'll say good night."

"Good night." Sleep tight. Don't let the bed bugs bite. Rosie had always said that when I was little. Rosie had taken care of me like a mother. And the whole time she'd never said a word.

In the bathroom, water ran, and then I heard the bedroom door close on her and Grandpop.

I waited, praying that Gary would want to take one of his midnight walks. I waited. Picked up the Nietzsche book and started reading, not really seeing the words. Funny writing, full of *hithertos*, *thees*, and *thous*, like the Bible. "Lo, I am weary of my wisdom, like the bee that hath gathered too much honey." Boy, you could say that again! I sat up and started paying more attention to the words. "Man is a rope . . . stretched . . . over an abyss. A dangerous crossing, a dangerous wayfaring, a dangerous looking-back." I read those words and they stung my eyes. That was me, a rope stretched across an abyss. And even while I was the rope, I was also the wayfarer, crossing over myself, wanting to look back.

I almost didn't hear it. Gary's white-sneakered step on the stairs. And then my ears became supertuned and I heard him go all the way down and out the front door. I could even hear the lock snap.

I knew Rosie would be awake, tossing and turning for his return, so I had to be quiet. I crept up to the third floor in my socks. I even knew where to avoid the creak in the fourth stair. His door was ajar.

My old desk lamp had been left on, spilling light across the gateleg desk. The notebook was what I wanted to look for first. Gary's secrets. He hadn't wanted me to look into that book. But if my mother's address wasn't in there, I would look through all his files, every single scrap of paper, just to make sure he was telling me the truth.

But the desk was a mess. I had to get it organized, or my search would be haphazard. And after, I'd have to mess things up again, so Gary wouldn't know. It would take time. I was shaking and sweating and I forced myself to get control. I went back and made sure the door was closed and then I started. A file of road maps, a street map of Kornkill. I put that aside. A file of what looked like reference letters. "I've known Gary Longman for the past three years and I can truthfully say . . ." I wondered if he had shown them to Rosie.

A pink file. The name *Dr. Kline* scrawled on the front. What the heck did Gary have on Kline? Inside, a letter: "Dear Gary . . . Best, Eliot Kline." I had to sit down. I read it all the way through.

Dear Gary:

Michael has been an enigma from the start. This indeed is not a simple case of juvenile delinquency as some would like so easily to explain. In fact, such terms are meaningless catchalls for an intricate problem like this.

I feel a sense of personal failure. The professional and clinical side of my nature resists. Yet how can I gaze into such liquid fathoms as his eyes and not be moved? Is this boy capable of murder? Have I done wrong in failing to reach him? If pressed to answer, I can only say he does not seem to fit into the orderly sense of things. But I am waxing on and this won't help you in your search.

Let me say that my analysis suggests strongly that Michael Thorn invented the man in the park for two reasons. The first, for expediency. To remove the burden of guilt from his own shoulders and put it onto someone else. The second reason is more interesting. Michael feels deprived of a father, which indeed has certainly been true. He feels anger toward this unknown father. Therefore, he creates a man—to become his father—and lays the blame for the murder on him, a symbolic acting out of the real father's actions of abandoning his mother.

I wish you well in your quest, my dear Gary, and I send my best wishes. Let me know as you uncover the facts. Our collaboration may yet produce a brilliant study of a murderer. Best,

Eliot Kline

I put the file down. My hand was shaking. I wanted to run out of the room, go screaming down the stairs. But I reminded myself: the notebook. I forced myself to keep looking for it. I overturned an empty coffee mug and it fell onto the carpet, making a soft thud. I froze. And there right under my hand was what I was looking for.

Pages filled with Gary's tiny handwriting. Some of it a bore. He described Kornkill as a sleepy, behind-the-times town on a river. Descriptions of Rosie and Grandpop. He called her beaky. Grandpop was "the man upstairs."

I flipped the pages. "Date: October 10. Interview: Mary Ann." First, stuff about the past, same thing he'd read to me. Elementary school. How she'd come from Chicago. Then there it was: the picnic. She'd told him all about the picnic but hadn't mentioned me. Just what happened.

"We were playing on the top of the wall. I'll never forget seeing Ginger falling down. It was like she was floating even though I know it was over in a second. I felt terrible for ages afterward, really guilty, because all I could think of at the time was that it could have been me."

I felt like kissing Mary Ann for not saying anything about me. I kissed the page of the notebook instead.

Next page there was the word NOTES in big letters, underlined a couple of times. Gary wrote:

When asked, M.A. says Michael was at the picnic but not present when they played on top of wall. Same wall in Monrovia Park—important. Is M.A. lying? Michael not implicated at the time. If M.A. knew something then, wouldn't want to tell now. She'd be accessory after the fact. What are the odds of person being in same place, with same occurrence, twice in his life? Saw Kline. He says too much of a long shot to be a coincidence, must be connection.

I slammed the notebook down and began to throw the files around, not really looking in a systematic way anymore. A whole pile of them slid onto the floor and it was like a signal, I began pushing everything off the table, shoving blindly out of spite, until the floor was littered and the table was bare except for the white coffee-mug rings and a single hardcover book.

It was a well-read book, finger-marked, dirty, annotated with Gary's cramped writing in all the margins, passages underlined, pages marked with crumbly, yellowish newspaper clippings.

In Cold Blood by Truman Capote. A true account of a multiple murder. It was a book about real people, the two guys who killed the Clutter family in Holcomb, Kansas. I'd seen the movie on television.

I knew what was going on, then. Gary wasn't writing a book to clear me of murder. He was writing a book about a murderer, just like Truman Capote, and the murderer was me.

I think I stood there a long time, holding the book in my hands, staring at the cover. I felt a draft on my back and I realized I was soaking with sweat.

"Find what you were looking for, Mike?" Gary said.

I turned around and it made me sick to look at him. "It would be a good idea if you got out of this house."

He had the stupidity to look surprised. "You don't understand," he started to say, but I pushed Capote's book hard into his stomach and he fell down, arms and legs flailing, like a big dirty bearded fly caught in a spider web.

"Get out," I said. "By tomorrow morning, I want you gone."

PART

III

21

In a nightmare you sometimes get a feeling: This can't be true. You tell yourself it's a dream. In the best nightmares you know it's a dream and you relax. You don't exactly enjoy the terror, but there's comfort in knowing that you'll wake up in the morning.

But there are nightmares that take you through the horror and drive it home, until you wake up, not in the morning, but in the dark of night, sweating, trembling, wondering who and where you are. For a few moments you stare into blood-red dark that slowly turns black again. A familiar room comes into focus as the dream recedes. But the horror stays.

And there are nightmares of a different kind. Bad dreams that are part of reality. That *are* reality.

When I was a kid in third grade, I was sitting in the back row and doodling on a scrap of notebook paper. I made a sticklike figure of a body, and on a whim, gave it two round circles for breasts. My first dirty picture. I thought it was funny and a little exciting. I showed it to the kid next to me. I think his name was Jerry. His eyes widened. "Gimme that," he said, and tore it from my hands. I was amazed that my picture had such power, flattered that Jerry seemed to want to devour it. But when he was finished looking, he stuck it in his pocket and said, "I'll tell on you."

The sudden and unexpected fear must have shown on my face. Jerry added, "Unless you bring me two candy bars a day."

I was scared. Scared the teacher would find out, that Rosie would find out. I'd made a dirty picture and the whole school would know. I was too terrified to eat supper that night, I couldn't sleep. But I must have drifted off. In the morning there were a few small moments of feeling fine until I remembered. The world came crashing down. Candy bars. Where was I going to get money for two candy bars a day?

I trembled through my breakfast, gagging on Rice Krispies. Reason began to prevail. I'd save my allowance, get money out of my piggy bank. I'd stockpile candy bars. But I didn't pass a candy store on the way to school, so this morning I would be empty handed. Would Jerry believe that I'd give him four bars tomorrow?

I must have looked pale. Rosie wanted to keep me home. A tempting way out. But still the problem of getting to the candy store. My mind was working overtime and I concocted a lie. Rosie, I need to bring some candy to school today because it's somebody's birthday and we're all supposed to chip in. But in the middle of my formulating it, the sun slipped in the window and spread a wide bar of warmth across the breakfast table, across my arms. And Grandpop shushed in in his slippers and tousled my hair. And suddenly it was over.

When I got to school and put my books inside my desk, Jerry said, "You bring the candy?" I shook my head. "No." That was all. He shrunk back a little. He never asked again. My first nightmare was over.

So I knew how to deal with blackmailers, but what about this nightmare now? It had been with me for almost a week. I still woke up in the morning and had that few seconds of peace until it hit me all over again. They had lied. I had a mother. I might be crazy. I was going crazy. Getting crazier.

So now I was going back, in my grandfather's Mercedes, on a trip to find out. I kept checking the mirror, making sure no cop was on my tail. What I didn't need was to get stopped for anything.

I was going back, walking on the rope stretched across the abyss. A dangerous crossing, a dangerous looking-back. I had Nietzsche on the seat next to me, but I didn't know what the hell he was talking about. Nietzsche is peachy. He's got this thing about metamorphosis. A spirit becomes a camel, a camel a lion, the lion a child. Who can make sense out of stuff like that? Seems to me it's a peculiar metamorphosis. If you were a lion, would you check it all in to become a child? If I were a lion, I'd stay that way. I wonder, do lions have nightmares? Maybe they dream of their enemies, of the sharp whipcrack of a bullet sinking into their chests. What a comedown: a lion, all those teeth, that big bushy mane, turned into a little baby sucking on a bottle of milk.

Maybe you have to go to college to understand Nietzsche. Maybe Wakefield understands it. I could ask him when he comes home for vacation. If I ever see Wakefield again.

If I ever see anybody again. On the road I think of cracking up. I think how sad everyone will be. Regretful. I think of the end. The End. Life is over. What do you become? A nothing. Like getting anesthetic and going nowhere. It won't be a nightmare in which you can think: This can't be true. You won't know you are you. It's horrible. I slow down and drive more carefully. I have no intention of cracking up.

"No, you are not the suicidal type," Dr. Kline, the shithead, had said, or was it Painter? One of the things they were right about, I'll give them credit. Didn't have to worry about me hanging myself like that one kid did.

I have this belief that I will stay intact when I die. I'll go on forever, no matter what, even though my body is gone. Rosie believes in the afterlife. She's not afraid of death because something better than life is coming up. Pearly gates and life everlasting. But I never heard any practical facts about it. What happens once you get through the gates? There's a lot more factual information about hell floating around than there is about life in heaven.

But what I want to know is, why am I here in the first place? Because I was once a camel who became a lion? I hate to sound like a cliché, but what's the point if you're only going to end up dead and forgetting who you are?

I shake my head to get rid of the death fear that has been coming on me like a stinking fog, seeping into my brain, making me go like a roller coaster inside.

I concentrate on the road, on keeping the speed limit, on my ultimate goal. I'm going to find my mother. When I find her, I'll understand everything.

But the roller coaster of fear comes down the chute from my brain, speed-bolting into my stomach, where it erupts into volcano. My heart feels like it's a bedspring, twanging in fright. I have to pull the car over onto the side of the road. Put my head down on the steering wheel. I feel exhausted, I haven't slept in days. It's all right, I comfort myself.

And then I begin to cry.

22

That morning after the scene with Gary, Rosie was at my bedroom door. "Michael! It's nine thirty, aren't you getting up?"

"No."

"Is it your head bothering you?"

"Yes."

"Do you want the doctor?"

"No."

I stayed huddled in bed, safe. But the night goblins were there, in the paint and plaster of my ceiling, in the fiendish voice outside my door. Reality. This wouldn't go away. Sick to my stomach from the realness of it.

"Something strange has happened," Rosie said. I wondered why she was talking through the door. For the first time, Rosie respecting my privacy. I wanted to laugh. What kind of strange thing could have happened? Could anything be stranger than what had happened to me last night?

"Come in," I told Rosie, even though I knew I'd want to scream at the sight of her. I pulled the covers up to my mouth.

Rosie stuck her head around, her nose sniffing

for indiscretion. "I can't understand it," she said. "Mr. Longman is gone."

"He always goes out early."

"No," Rosie said, pulling an envelope out of the pocket of her housecoat. "He left me a letter and a whole month's rent." She held the envelope like it was something dangerous. "He says he was called out of town unexpectedly."

"Well, I guess he had to go." I felt glad, relieved.

"But he's left his things up there," Rosie said, looking skyward and wrinkling her nose. Her lips tightened. "It will take more than a month's rent to get that room back in order."

"Throw his stuff out."

"We can't do that!" Rosie was shocked. "What I don't understand is why he sneaked out in the night. Leaving this letter on the telephone! I might have missed it." Absently, she brushed at the dust on my desktop. "And the chain was off all night!"

"Nothing happened to us."

She peered at me. "You all right?"

"Sure."

"I'll phone Linny."

"He won't expect me," I said. I saw Aunt Heva's rabbit eyes. Protecting me from the truth. Protecting herself from the truth. Who would be the one person Aunt Heva wouldn't tell on? Was it Lindsay who had come back and tried to kill me? It had to be Lindsay.

Rosie began fluffing up my pillows, trying to

make me comfortable. What did I want for breakfast? She would fix me a tray. Cinnamon toast?

"Remember how I always made you cinnamon toast when you were little? You liked it cut into triangles. You always said, 'Rosie, it doesn't taste the same if it isn't cut that way.' "

I just couldn't hold it in anymore, listening to her babble. I screamed at her to stop.

Rosie jumped back against the wall as if the sound had propelled her there. Grandpop came running from his room. "What the blazes . . ." His face at the door was alert, worried, pale.

I looked at them. Rosie terrified, Grandpop annoyed. Yet behind their eyes was concern for me. Oh, God, what do I do now? Why am I praying?

"It's a concussion," Rosie said, her voice a trembling whisper. "I better call—"

And I screamed again. It was a man-scream, aaaaaaaaaah, better than in a horror movie. A pain scream, a fear scream, a hate scream.

"No. I just want to tell you . . ." My chest felt like it was full of cement. I could hardly breathe the words out. I told myself: Don't you dare, don't you even think about losing your voice now. "I wanted to tell you . . . I know. I know. I *know!*"

"Know what, Mickey dear?" Rosie said.

I laughed. Grandpop was edging back out the door, planning action. Michael Thorn had gone off the deep end again, needed help. He was probably thinking: What the hell is the number of the school, who is the psychiatrist? Come back, take him away.

"I know about my mother."

Rosie sat down in my desk chair with a thump, like she'd been pushed. Her legs sprawled out like a rag doll's. "Holy Mother of God," she said.

Grandpop came forward in a menacing way. "What are you talking about? What do you know?"

"You lied."

"Understand this, son, understand this, it was necessary. . . ." But Rosie had recovered and began shushing him not to say anything. "Let him speak first," she told Grandpop. "Let's find out first." Wily Rosie.

They looked at me, waiting.

"My mother's alive, not dead like you told me all these years."

"Now, Mickey, there were reasons . . ." Rosie began to say.

"Like the fact she was in Amber Knoll?" I asked. "Where is she now?"

Grandpop slumped, looked like he'd been slapped, all the piss and vinegar gone out of him.

"We don't know," Rosie said quietly. She was calm again. "That's the God's honest truth."

"God, ha! Why should I believe a couple of liars?"

"What she says is so," Grandpop said.

"The people at the hospital were rude," Rosie went on. "So much as said we were a bad influence. 'It's time you let Mrs. Thorn live her own life,' they told me when I inquired where she'd gone. Mrs. Thorn my foot!" Rosie sniffed. "Mrs. Nobody."

Grandpop grabbed out and his hands clamped around Rosie's wrists. "Shut up!" he snarled. All the times he'd told Rosie to keep quiet it had never sounded so vicious. It shocked Rosie into silence for a moment. Her face turned bright red and tears exploded from her eyes. Grandpop let go of her and she rubbed her arms.

"He's old enough to know!" she spat at him. She turned to me. "Allie was never anything more than Miss. She never had a proper husband with a marriage." Rosie fumbled around, looking for a tissue. The box on my night table was empty. She searched her pockets and pulled out Gary's letter. She mopped at her face with it. "You're a bastard, Michael."

"What kind of a thing is that to say?" Grandpop shouted. "Don't you have any sense left in your head?"

"It's the God's honest truth," Rosie said.

"Nobody speaks in terms like that anymore," Grandpop yelled.

"Look it up in the dictionary!" Rosie screamed back at him.

"There are better ways of saying things," Grandpop said, more quietly. "Ways to soften the blow."

"Didn't you hear him?" Rosie shrieked. "He called us liars. He doesn't want any blows softened anymore. He wants to know the truth. I'm just telling him."

It was suddenly as if I was out of my body,

watching a scene from a play. Rosie and Grandpop standing like wizened scarecrows. The tendons in Grandpop's neck almost bursting, his Adam's apple bobbing. Rosie weeping and raving, a flaming Celtic fury of red hair and cheeks. And me, lying in bed, the covers pulled up to my chin, a talking corpse.

"This is ludicrous," I said.

Grandpop gave a sound—not unlike the violins of my homecoming, but instead of a weeping this was a warped, twisted laugh. "Just what we need," he said, "is a sense of humor."

"Sick humor," Rosie said. Her cheeks were paling to their normal color. She noticed she had been wiping her nose on Gary's letter and she stuffed it back into her pocket.

"If you understood the facts, you would find it in your heart to forgive us," she said to me. "Can you forgive us?"

"I haven't heard the facts," I said in a detached way, sounding cool. "Anyway, I don't forgive liars." I hadn't really wanted to say that, but it came out anyway. I wasn't up to forgiveness. I wanted them to go away and leave me alone.

"Don't be stupid," Grandpop said. "Grow up." He took Rosie by the arm, but gently this time. "Let him be for a while. When he decides to act like a man, he can get out of bed and get dressed and come downstairs to talk to us. This isn't the end of the world."

I didn't make a move for a long time. But finally I had to get up to pee. And once I was up, it seemed logical to get dressed. And then I decided to go downstairs because I was hungry.

I don't know if it had anything to do with acting like a man. My anger was subsiding and turning into worry. The question of my mother's and my own sanity was pushing at my heart.

Grandpop had made a supreme concession and was waiting for me in Rosie's needlepoint-and-velvet parlor. Although the bars of the electric fire had been turned on, the room was still cold and formal. As if on cue Rosie appeared with a tray of tea and cinnamon toast. This was, I could tell, a great occasion. She poured tea methodically; there was a clinking of china and half-stifled gurgles as we downed our first sips.

"Linny says not to worry, he can manage for as long as it takes you to get better," Rosie said for openers.

Grandpop crunched a piece of cinnamon toast and the sugar cascaded down onto his trousers. Rosie had cut the toast into triangles. On principle I refused to take a piece.

"Don't blame your grandfather," Rosie began. "I talked him into it. He was against it, so it's my fault. I never had a child, you see, and you were like my own." Her lower lip trembled, but a warning look from Grandpop made her get control. "I wanted to be your mother. Your *only* mother."

"Nonsense!" Grandpop cried, flicking cinnamon and sugar off his knees. "I told Allie I would never forgive her and I haven't. She got herself into trouble and refused to listen to reason. She always did what she wanted to do, she paid me no mind. Wasn't interested in her father's advice. Wouldn't have it. You don't want a father, I said to her, then you're no daughter of mine."

"You don't mean that," Rosie told him. "Not deep down. You've been hurt and you're angry. But you still love her."

"Don't tell me who I love!" Grandpop roared.

And so my past and my future dissolved over tea and toast as they bickered, dredging up old grievances and picking and scraping at their resentments. They didn't even know I was there.

I helped Rosie bring the tea tray back to the kitchen. Grandpop went upstairs and shut himself in with his bugs. Rosie washed the china meticulously, turning the cups over and over under the tap. I found some bread and cheese. I got out the hot mustard and began to make myself a sandwich.

"Why did she go crazy?" I asked.

Rosie stopped rinsing the cups. She dried her hands. She sat down at the kitchen table and made me put my sandwich down, and she reached across the checkered tablecloth and took my hands. I felt the dryness of her skin. Her fingers were cold, although they had been in hot soapy water moments before.

"Crazy is a nonsensical term. She had a nervous breakdown. So many bad things happened. She was high-strung and headstrong. Got involved with a man and got pregnant. Never would tell us who. We urged her to arrange a marriage, but she refused. She had such silly ideas, Mickey, I'm embarrassed to tell you. You know it was that period of hippies and she wanted to act like a love child. They pretended that all you had to do to make things right in the world was make love not war. Now, wouldn't that be nice if it was true?" Rosie gave a sad smile. She wouldn't let go of my hands.

"Pop was in a temper long before the pregnancy. Everything she did was wrong. Getting pregnant was the straw that broke the camel's back. But still, he tried to help. We tried to do what was best, but it was no use with her." Rosie's fingers squeezed tight. "You have to understand, Mickey, I didn't steal you from her. You were neglected. I couldn't stand by and watch that. Maybe it was a sin, but I did what I thought was best, for your own good, Michael."

"But maybe not for my mother's good."

Rosie released my hands. "Oh, what would you know about it?" she snapped. "I had to take you away from her, and after that she went downhill. Nobody knows exactly why."

"I do. She missed me."

Rosie sighed. "The young will believe what they like."

"I'm going to find her," I said.

Rosie stared past me. She seemed to be looking into the past. I expected her to cry again, but instead her face darkened and she slapped her hand down angrily on the table. The newly washed cups rattled on the drainboard.

"Ungrateful," she said. "You and your grandfather. I was the one who did something for the good. Pop would have let you die with her. I saved you."

"God, Rosie . . ."

She jumped up and came around to me, put her arms around me, pulled me into her until I could feel her bones against my bones.

"No, that's unfair. He loves you. But her, your mother, he never got over that. I remember he came home one afternoon and tore through the house, destroying all her things, annihilating every trace of her. It was worse than if she'd died. It was like she had never existed at all. Wouldn't you go crazy if your father disowned you like that?"

"Sure," I said, muffled in Rosie's embrace. "I would. It's exactly how I feel. It's exactly what my father did to me."

23

It was later that afternoon the doorbell rang. Rosie called to me: "Answer it, please, Michael, I'm too upset." Rosie had been lying down for over an hour, something she almost never did, even when she had the flu.

I had a dread it would be Gary at the door. I might kill him. But when I opened the door, I saw Suds, the taxi driver.

He was standing, giving the impression of leaning, a cigarette burning itself down to a stub between his stained fingers.

"Hi ya," he said. "I come for Mr. Longland's stuff."

I must have looked like a statue because Suds shifted so that he leaned in the opposite direction. "Mr. Longland? He sent me to pick up his stuff." Suds flicked the butt out over the porch rail, where it landed on the lawn. He pulled out a piece of paper and held it at arm's length, squinting his eyes. He read, in a voice like a school report: "One tape deck, one ampleeflyer, one graphic whatever, two speakers, one box books, one box miscellaneous household." He folded the paper back up and beamed at me.

"Okay. Come in. It's upstairs."

Surprisingly, there was no dread going into Gary's room. He had taken all his papers and clothes, but his books were still lined up on the windowsill and the toaster oven and electric coffee-pot were under the bed. Suds looked around the room with dismay.

"This here ain't packed up," he said.

I shrugged. I didn't care whether Gary ever saw his one tape deck, two speakers, et cetera, again.

"I ain't no moving man," said Suds. "I'm doing a favor."

"Sorry I can't help you," I said. "Maybe you should talk to Mr. Long*land* about it."

This cheered Suds up. "You're right. That's what I'll do. After all, I ain't no moving man."

"No, you're no moving man," I agreed. Suds went back down the stairs, whistling.

"Maybe I'll be back," he said at the door, looking a little undecided. "I mean, I can't take that stuff as is, right?"

"Right," I told him.

"I'll see you, then," he said.

I watched him go down the path and climb into his black taxi. I thought how worried I'd been about Suds that first day I came home. I gave him a friendly wave good-bye.

Rosie managed to recover in time to prepare dinner. I saw her popping Tylenol at the kitchen sink. Vaguely, I worried that all this emotional upset would make her really sick. I realized Rosie wasn't young anymore. Neither was Grandpop. Maybe they'd die and it would be my fault for kicking up such a fuss about the past.

Going a little soft, aren't you kid? the voice in my head asked. Yeah, maybe. But suppose Gary had never told me about my mother, and suppose I had gone all through life not knowing, what would have been the difference? The fact that my mother was alive wasn't even connected to the reason Gary was here. The night in Monrovia Park had nothing to do with my mother. *Suppose the earth was flat?* the voice said.

By tacit agreement none of us mentioned the room upstairs while we were eating dinner. We were waiting for it to take care of itself.

While we were eating, the phone rang. You know, it was funny how we could sit down at the table and dish up food, like everything was normal. But when the phone rang, we jumped a mile.

I went to answer. Subtly, something *had* changed. Now it was me who was answering doors and phones, like Rosie and Grandpop were receding into the background.

I picked up the phone warily, wondering if life had any more big surprises in store for me. But I heard Mary Ann's voice on the line.

"Hi, Michael, I hope you don't mind I called?"

"Why should I mind?"

"Some people think it's wrong for a girl to call a guy."

"That's a crock," I said—too dead serious, as I realized too late, because there had been a joking lilt to her voice.

"Look, I wondered . . . what're you doing? Want to go out for pizza?"

"I'd like to," I stammered. Here I was eating dinner with two old fogeys. I felt like a clod. "But . . ."

"Don't worry about driving, I'll pick you up."

I found myself bristling at the familiarity. She had it all arranged. Somehow it reminded me of Lindsay. Or maybe anger was still poised on the edge of my nerves, so that it flared up for a moment irrationally and had nothing to do with Mary Ann. But too long a pause went by before I answered her.

"Well, look, I guess you're busy," she said, and her voice was like delicate crystal ready to break.

"I'm sorry," I started to say, sounding like limp spaghetti. I was sorry I had been angry for no reason, and now I was feeling angry that I had to feel sorry. "I'm eating dinner, for God's sake," I wanted to yell at her. "How can I go out for pizza at a time like this?"

"Don't worry about it," she said briskly. The crystal fell, shattered, tinkled away. I was still trying to explain when I realized she'd hung up.

Catatonic, that's what I was. I hadn't said anything I wanted to say. I liked Mary Ann! I'd wanted to see her again. But I couldn't find the proper feelings inside me right now. I felt dead inside. Except for the anger. I had no trouble getting in touch with that. I stood in the hall for a moment, debating whether I should call back to apologize. Then Rosie called from the dining room. "Michael, your food's getting cold."

"Fuck food!" I yelled, and grabbed my old sweater from the front hall closet. I ran outside, ran down Carhart Street—I didn't know where I was running, but it felt good to be getting away from something.

I ran all the way out Monrovia Boulevard, was heading for town in a blind sort of way, when my head began to throb so bad I had to stop. I sat down on the low stone wall bordering somebody's lawn. The house was lighted up, oblongs of yellow spilling out across the grass, almost touching me. I could see people moving around inside, carrying plates, probably finishing dinner, just like Rosie and Grandpop would be doing. I wondered if I had ever gone into this particular house to sit in the living room and listen for voices to tell me the answers to questions I didn't even know. The stone was cold and damp, creeping right through my jeans. "You'll get hemorrhoids," I could hear Rosie say, a far-distant past voice in a kaleidoscope of visions. Rosie, my *only* mother, that's what she wanted to be. That's what I thought she was and I hadn't minded until yesterday. It wasn't fair to cancel her out. Rosie was the one who had been there, bringing me a vomit pan in the night, rubbing my almost-frostbitten toes when I stayed out at the skating pond too long, worrying about me going on the camping trip, checking my trick-or-treat boodle for pins and razor blades, protecting me from mean teachers, school bullies, kidnappers, poisoners, blackmailers.

Give me a break, bleeding heart, the voice in my head said. Okay. Rosie forcing me to wear short pants when everyone else wore long trousers, Rosie refusing to buy me more than one pair of jeans, Rosie coming to Open School Night in her ratty fur hat and beaver coat, making me want to die.

I couldn't hate her. I was still dead inside. I was mad at her for lying to me, but I couldn't find any live, hot hate.

The people in the house pulled the drapes across the windows and I saw the bluish flickering light of a TV set turned on. I thought of them in there, one big happy family, talking and laughing with each other, feeling like they belonged.

And suddenly, it seemed to me I almost had the answer to why I went inside all those houses. I was looking for the thing I'd lost. I was looking for that kind of family, with a real mother and a real father. I wanted to be their real child. I remember hearing other kids yelling, "Daddy!" Me saying "Grandpop." "Where's your father?" some kid once asked me. I said my father was away in the war. "When's he coming home?" the kid persisted. I said I didn't know. Maybe soon. Maybe any day now. Probably. But the kid looked at me sadly and murmured, "I guess he got killed, huh?"

It seemed like a good idea, so for a while I pretended my dad had been killed in Vietnam. This was a whole lot easier than telling them: "I haven't got a clue who my father was."

Yeah, are you listening, Dr. Shitface Kline? I know the reason now. Maybe I should go down to the juvenile court and tell them, too. You want to know why I went into people's houses? I was looking for my parents. You can't blame a kid for that, can you? Any lost kid is going to search for his family. Any poor lost dopey sad kid is going to look high and low for his mommy and daddy. It seems . . . it seems like that sort of thing is an inalienable right.

I got scared for a moment because I was sort of gasping and I was afraid I might have really given my speech out loud. But the house behind me was quiet. Nothing around me stirred.

I felt better. A little feeling was coming back, nipping at me with a chance for a little happiness. I felt like I wanted to talk to Mary Ann.

Cripes, I didn't even know where she lived. Had to think. Get a phone book. I felt in my pockets and found a couple of quarters. Call information. I went looking for a phone. Hoping she wouldn't be too pissed to talk to me. Hoping she'd still be home.

"Hlavadic," I told the operator, but I had to spell it, I never could pronounce that name. The operator took a year. How many Hlavadics could be in Kornkill? Finally, I got the number.

When a man answered, I stifled the urge to

hang up. "Could I speak to Mary Ann?" I heard him call, "Emmay, telephone!"

Emmay. M.A. Gary's tight little handwritten words flashed in my mind.

"Hi, Emmay, it's Emmtee," I said. My voice was shaky nervous.

"Who?" she said. That sweet, uncertain voice. "What's empty?"

"It's me, Michael. I'm sorry about before."

"Are you okay?"

"Sure I'm okay. Why shouldn't I be okay? I'm standing on Monrovia Boulevard, freezing my ass, talking to you in a telephone booth that stinks of pee."

"I'll come over. I'll pick you up. Don't move," Mary Ann said.

"I'm all right, really. I'd appreciate your coming to get me. As a matter of fact, I never finished my dinner, so we can go for pizza after all." I gulped some air. "Shit, I just want to see you."

"I'll be right there." I gave her directions. She hung up, but I kept the phone stuck to my ear, breathing in the stink of urine and trying to catch my breath. You can talk, I told myself. You can keep on talking. You're not going to lose your voice again. You're not going to lose anything again. I kept on talking into the dead telephone, just gibberish, just to keep my voice working. I talked until Mary Ann's car pulled up alongside the curb and her wide, concerned eyes looked up at me.

24

The memory of that night with Mary Ann circled me like a halo, as protecting as her arms had been around me.

We didn't do much talking. She drove out on the point and parked the car facing the river, and we watched the twinkling lights from the opposite shore for a while, just holding hands. And it was like Mary Ann absorbed me through her fingers, knew what was on my mind without my even saying it. I told her a little about my mother. I didn't think I was showing much emotion about it, just relating how Gary had known, how Rosie and Grandpop had lied for my own good, and then Mary Ann put her finger to my lips and said, "Sssssh" and she slipped her arms around me and I was kissing her lips, her eyes, her hair.

And I felt very frightened, afraid of what would happen, remembering against my will that scene in Murworth's Tomb with Lindsay. I felt like I was walking on ice, that at any moment the spell would be broken and Mary Ann would lean back, light a cigarette, rasp at me with a voice full of innuendos.

But it wasn't like that. There was no rush, no

hurry, just being together, feeling each other's warmth. It was a feeling like I'd never experienced before, a lustrous bath of light that dazzled me, and I had to close my eyes against the glare.

I thought: Do I love you? But I was still slowly moving across that layer of thin ice, still afraid I wouldn't make it to the other side. I didn't know what she wanted of me. To keep on kissing her, caressing her, to go on and on to make love to her?

Her flesh seemed to melt into me, until I couldn't tell the difference between me or her. I wanted her so much. And I wanted it to be all right. I wanted to do it right. And yet I knew we could stop and it wouldn't matter because there were a thousand days and nights stretching out ahead of me, filled with Mary Ann. "Is it all right?" I asked. "Is it all right?"

"Michael," she whispered to me. "We better not."

"It's okay," I said. I didn't want her to worry. I didn't want her to even think I wouldn't do what she said. We were half-lying on the front seat of the car, and now I sat up and she absently straightened her clothes and patted her hair, all the time looking in the rearview mirror. I picked up on something. "What's the matter?"

"Just a feeling, probably nothing. I really came here so we could talk." Through the night I saw her smile and she reached out. "We didn't do much talking. . . ."

I wanted to hold her again, but she started the car. "Forgive me, I got this hunch."

And she backed the car up and turned, and the headlights beamed into the night and caught the edge of a bumper, a quick glint of a hubcap shielded by the trees. Mary Ann stepped on the gas and we were off the access road in a flash, moving across Railroad Avenue, crossing Main Street. Mary Ann took the long way around to get to Monrovia Boulevard. Nobody followed us.

"I had this feeling we were being watched," she said. "Is that crazy?"

"Nothing's too crazy to be true anymore."

"No . . . it is crazy. Probably somebody else parked, just like us."

"Something must have been there to make you uneasy," I said.

"It was, well . . . it's a little embarrassing— you'll think it's awful of me." She gave me a sheepish smile. I reached for her hand.

"Come on, what? Tell me," I said.

"In the middle of it, while we were, you know . . . I couldn't help it, my eyes were open. I thought I saw someone walking around the car, looking in."

A shiver went through me. I felt the memory of that graveyard pain at the back of my head. "For real?"

She nodded. "Who do you think it was?" She sounded worried, scared. I didn't want her to be scared.

"Probably Charlie Melville," I said. "He's been checking up on me."

She relaxed. But it hadn't looked like Charlie's police car in the trees. But then, I hadn't got a really good look. Or it could have been that graveyard person, sneaking up on me again. Lindsay? How could it have been Lindsay?

And then another possibility came rushing into my mind. A much better possibility, and I felt dumb I hadn't ever thought of it before. The shivers in my spine turned to ice cubes. It could have been the man in the park. Gary was spouting his mouth off all around town, letting everybody know the murder was still on my mind. The man in the park wasn't safe anymore now that I was back in town. And if I were him and I'd murdered a girl, I'd want to be real sure that there weren't any witnesses around to tell about my crime.

"You're looking worried," Mary Ann said. "You don't really think it was Charlie Melville, do you?"

"Sure, sure I do," I said. But already, Mary Ann knew me better. She pulled up in front of No. 5 Carhart Street. I glanced at my watch and realized I'd been gone for hours. It was past midnight.

"Never did get that pizza," I said.

Mary Ann cut the ignition and doused the lights. The porch light was on, waiting for me to come home. The rest of the house was dark.

"Michael," Mary Ann said, coming close, putting her arms around me again. "You don't have to say anything. But if you want to tell me, I'm here to listen to it all."

You know how they say the dam broke? It's the best way to say it, that's what happened. I told her everything, from beginning to end. I even told her my last, most terrifying thought about the man in the park.

"So you think Lindsay knocked you on the head in the graveyard, because she was mad at being rejected?" Mary Ann asked after I'd finished.

"She seems the most likely person for Aunt Heva to shield. And she was in the vicinity. And she was furious at me."

"And you think whoever might have been spying on us tonight was the man you saw push the girl over the wall in Monrovia Park?"

"A good possibility. I know Lindsay wouldn't be out scouting around the point. I mean, how could she even know I was out with you? It had to be someone with a car, who followed me from my house, saw me phone you, and saw me get into your car."

"I don't know," Mary Ann said. "I can't help feeling it has to be the same person both times. It's hard to believe that two different people are after you."

"But it has to be someone Aunt Heva knows. Otherwise why would she lie? Lindsay was at the graveyard, but it's a real long shot that Lindsay was at the point tonight. And anyway, Lindsay wouldn't have had anything to do with the girl's murder."

Mary Ann looked at me funny. "But," she said in her soft voice, "Lindsay was the very person you were meeting at the park that night."

"Oh, come on," I said. My whole body was revolting at the thought. "Look, I saw a *man,* not Lindsay. She was fourteen years old; what do you think, she got herself into a jealous rage because she thought I was two-timing her?"

"Lindsay could be sick," Mary Ann said evenly.

"Lindsay was home that night, her father wouldn't let her go out."

"Her father was the one who said you were alone at the park. He'd want to protect his daughter, wouldn't he?"

"Oh, Jesus," I said. My hands were shaking. I steadied them on the dashboard. Then I smacked it, so hard the car bounced. "It was a man! I saw a man."

"Okay," Mary Ann said. She took my hands in hers.

Disguises. Lies. Disguises. I hadn't even known the girl who was killed. She was from Melford. Worked in an insurance company.

"This is turning into a freak show," I said.

"Look, let's go back and separate the two things. You're probably right, it wasn't the same person. Probably Lindsay gave you a bash because she was mad, but she wasn't trying to kill you. And her aunt doesn't want to say it was her, that's logical. Tonight could have been anybody. It's all my fault for even bringing it up. It could have been some pervert who likes getting his rocks off as a peeping Tom. It could have been Charlie Melville, like you said. He's been known to give kids a scare out on the point, just for kicks. It could even have been your great friend Gary, spying on you for his book. That makes sense, doesn't it?"

"Yeah." I had to admit it did. I wouldn't put it past Gary. "I think I'm getting paranoid, just like Lindsay said." I tried to laugh, but only a croak came out.

The hall lights went on in the house. Rosie was up and ready to pounce. "I better go in," I said. "I left in a bit of a hurry. They're worried about me. I think I put them through hell today."

But Mary Ann looked grim. "You're the one who's been through hell, Michael," she said.

I kissed her one last time. I wanted to tell her how I felt. But I just got out of the car. She rolled down the window and blew me another kiss. I started up the path.

"Hey, Michael," she called in a whispery voice. I turned around. "I think I love you."

Before I could answer she was gone and again I watched the little red blinker at the corner, and then the car was out of sight.

25

Mary Ann in my mind made it all seem easier. I didn't have a clue what I was going to do about anything, I didn't know where my life was going, and the job at the graveyard was as good as over. Rosie, Grandpop, Linny, Aunt Heva—they were crumbling away, they were losing their shape in my life. I knew I had to make plans, but I put it off. When I felt the fear and trembling moving on in, I hoisted up a vision of Mary Ann in my mind.

And then I got a phone call from Gary that changed everything. The phone rang in the late afternoon and I picked it up and heard his pushy, know-it-all voice crawling like a worm in my ear.

"Hey, Mike, I'm glad you answered. Listen, don't hang up on me, I got to talk to you."

I said nothing. There was breathing between us on the line.

"You still there?" he asked.

"So talk."

"Listen, I understand how you feel. You read my notes, right? The letter from Kline, right? You saw everything?"

"I saw everything."

"Well, you picked a bad time. You should've waited a couple of days. I was in the process of revising. I don't agree with Kline anymore."

"I don't give a rat's ass."

"You should. Because if I don't agree with him that means I have a helluva good reason not to. Kline subsidized me, kid. To disagree with him means kicking the gift horse in the teeth."

"I'm wetting my pants I'm so overcome with joy."

"Oh, cut the crap," Gary said.

"That's easy enough, I'll hang up."

"Wait, wait!" Gary cried. "Let's meet. I want to talk to you. I have serious things to say."

"I don't ever want to see your lousy face again."

"Okay. I know when I'm beat. I'll send it in the mail."

"Send what in the mail?"

"Your mother's address."

"What is this, your idea of a joke?"

"Did I say I had serious business? What do you think I've been doing all this time? Did I leave a note I'd be out of town? Did I say I was your friend?"

"Shut up!" I yelled into the phone.

There was a repentant silence. Then Gary asked tentatively, "So should I send it in the mail?"

I wanted that address like crazy, so much I felt like jumping through the phone for it. But I didn't want to see Gary. There was something lousy about it, like I'd suddenly be beholden to him when it was he who'd caused all the pain. Anyhow, it could just be another one of his tricks.

"What's the matter with you giving it to me right now, over the phone?"

"Oh," he said, and his voice sounded deflated, a little of the know-it-allness gone out of it. I was glad. I used Rosie's gold pencil to write what he told me on the notepad she kept next to the phone. Star Route—Box 40. Up in a place called Emmiston, about a hundred miles from here. "She's going by the name Allison Jones."

I knew I should say thanks, but the word stuck in my throat. "How'd you find out?" I asked instead.

"Friends in high places," Gary bragged. "Kline can still come in handy."

A bastard to the end, I thought. I didn't even say good-bye, I just hung up.

I didn't have to think twice to make up my mind. But I waited until I heard Grandpop was in his room before I went to tell Rosie.

"I'm going," I said. "I'm going to see my mother. I know where she is now."

Rosie looked yellowish and old. She didn't protest or ask me where, she seemed resigned, as if she knew I wouldn't tell her.

"I'm going to take the Mercedes," I said.

"No, no, you can't," she said, coming to life.

"I'm going to. If you or Grandpop want to call the cops, it'll be on your head."

"I wasn't thinking of the police," Rosie said,

flustered. "The car is in no condition to run. It's been up on blocks for years, you know that."

Shit, I thought, what do I do now? Take a bus? Hitchhike? I needed a car, in case my mother wasn't even in Emmiston, in case I ran into a dead end, which was possible since I was working on Gary's word and that hadn't meant much in the past. I couldn't ask Mary Ann to drive me. I didn't know how long I'd be gone. And seeing my mother resurrected from the dead? That was something a guy had to do on his own.

I knew Grandpop. He wouldn't let his car go to seed even if he didn't drive it anymore.

"I'll take it down," I said to Rosie.

"I don't know anything about cars," Rosie said, wringing her hands. "What am I going to tell Pop?" But in the meantime she was fumbling in one of the kitchen drawers where she keeps all her coupons and receipts. She came up with the key.

I went out to the garage. The Mercedes, looking like a big black beetle, was sitting on oak blocks. It was typical of Grandpop that it was clean and shiny. I felt sure it would run once it was down. But for a fleeting moment I almost wished Gary was still around, so I could steal his car instead.

Use your head, I told myself. I got the jack and wheeled it out, braced it at the back, and pumped. When the car was raised just enough, I pulled the blocks out. They weighed a son of a gun. Then I lowered her down. The tires probably needed air, but they looked in good condition. Feeling excited, I got in and turned the key in the ignition. Nothing happened.

It wasn't a matter of gas, the engine didn't even cough. Dead battery. If I'd been at Kornkill High instead of up the river for two years, I'd probably know all about cars. I might even have my own. But instead I knew all about doing laundry, and how to run an institution-size dishwasher, and how to make sponge cake for two hundred. I could probably run a hotel, but I couldn't start a damn car.

I raised the hood and looked in, hoping the answer might jump out at me. I had my head under there when I heard someone come into the garage.

"Got to connect the battery," my grandfather said. He came around the side of the car, patting it fondly. "A wonderful machine. Nothing in the world like a Mercedes-Benz." He was smiling. "The best investment I ever made."

"I don't understand" was all I could say.

"Had a daughter who wouldn't listen to reason. Did what she wanted to do. Now it looks like her son is taking after her. He's bound and determined to do what he wants and an old man's advice won't stop him." He looked at me with his pale blue eyes and I thought: My mother's eyes are darker. "I don't want to lose you, too," he said.

Some kind of feeling of gratitude was filling me up, killing me with kindness. "But I don't have a license, I could get into trouble," I said, almost thinking Grandpop had gone senile, didn't know

what he was doing. I didn't want to fool him, tell him
any lies.

"I don't approve!" he thundered, and his
words echoed to the roof of the garage. "But," he
continued more quietly, "if you're determined to
steal my car, I want her taken care of. And I expect
her back, in the same condition as she left."

We had a cold supper in the kitchen. Rosie was
too nervous to cook. She thought she felt the flu
coming on. She packed me sandwiches. Grandpop
had turned morose. He complained about eating
cold food in the cold winter. I was glad he was in a
bad mood. It made it easier. In the garage I had
almost died, not knowing how to say thank-you, not
even knowing if he wanted me to. Grandpop and I,
we didn't have enough practice talking to each
other. It wasn't like with Mary Ann. How do you say
stuff like "I love you" to your grandfather?

He went upstairs right after supper. "Watch
yourself," he said, and he was gone. I think Rosie
breathed a sigh of relief, just like me. But I wished
she'd go away somewhere, too. I wanted to just
leave. No big farewells, no teary good-byes. I
packed some stuff and was planning to slip out, but
Rosie was there waiting in the darkened hall.

"Mickey, are you ever coming back?"

"Have to," I said, trying to make a joke. "Got to
return Grandpop's car."

We stood there looking at each other. I tried to
summon up the courage to kiss her. I told myself it
was the least I could do. I told myself I was a real

creep, not being able to show a little affection. Rosie and Grandpop were helping me and I was like a stone. When I did take the plunge and leaned forward to peck her cheek, Rosie decided to do the same thing. We bumped heads and I ended up kissing her nose. I laughed, she laughed, to cover up.

"Good luck, Mickey," she said. "Godspeed."

God better speed me, I thought, driving out of town. I had only the gas that had been in the can for the lawn mower. But I couldn't risk stopping in town. Charlie Melville would like nothing better than to nail me on this.

I must have gone ten miles up the parkway when I saw the lighted sign of a service station looming up through the trees. I pulled off at the next exit. A kid about my own age came out and I told him to fill it up. "Yes, sir," he said, and I had to give a laugh.

As he pumped gas, I went over to a phone that was hanging on a pole under a bright neon light. I dialed Mary Ann's number, made the call collect. I told her where I was going.

"All set, sir," the kid called as he screwed the gas cap back on.

"Gotta go," I said to Mary Ann.

Now or never, I thought. And I said it. Finally. "I love you." Finally. I'd told her. I'd told someone. I'd said the words out loud.

26

A young girl in a sheepskin jacket was standing in front of the farmhouse, her long hair blowing across her face. She smoothed it away as she watched me coming, her face curious, a little puzzled.

A cat wove itself in and out between her ankles, its big fluffy tail arched. Some dry leaves scattered in a gust of wind and scuffled against the car. The farm looked humble, a little neglected, but there were pink roses still blooming along the split-rail fence. I sailed smoothly over the bumps and ruts of the dirt track. There's no car like a Mercedes-Benz.

"I'm looking for the Jones farm," I said to her, and stopped at the end of the track. I had been looking for an hour, in spite of the explicit directions I'd got from at least three people in the Emmiston post office. Directions would have been fine if the roads had signs, but I got lost in a jumble of unmarked country lanes.

"This is Jones," the girl said. She walked toward me, still holding her hair back with one hand. The cat followed at her heels. When she got to the fence, she leaned on the top rail and the cat jumped up and rubbed itself against her thick brown gloves.

I saw she was not a young girl at all; age showed around her eyes and mouth. Yet, when she smiled at me, she became the girl again. I stared into her eyes.

"I'm looking for Allison Jones," I said.

"That's me."

My mother. This was my mother. The moon-blue eyes and the hair that used to tickle me. My heart thumped with recognition made from dreams, but she looked at me as if I were a complete stranger.

She stood calmly surveying me, waiting for me to state my business. She looked in control of herself and her world. Now that I was at the end of my journey, I didn't know what to say. I sat there, the Mercedes purring, the cat and the woman peering at me, and I was tongue-tied.

I had performed all kinds of visions of this meeting in my mind; embarrassed that some of them were really corny, the kind of stuff in a TV ad. Lots of running toward each other, weeping and shouting. And sometimes I had been real afraid of too much shock, too much joy. But this girl-woman didn't look as if she could be shocked. She looked as if she had all the time in the world to spend waiting on the other side of the fence while I figured out how to state my business. She scratched the cat behind its ear.

"I'm Michael Thorn," I said, not being able to think of anything else.

Her expression never changed, but in slow motion she began to fall, going down with her hand still on the cat's ear, pulling the cat with her. It let out a strident meow and lost its balance. It clung, swinging, to the railing, as my mother sank down onto her knees. Her hair fell in front of her face.

I jumped out of the car.

"I'm all right," she said, holding me off, keeping me at a distance. I waited until she got up, hauling herself on the fence. She brushed her hair away again, looked at me with tearless eyes. "My son Michael Thorn?"

I nodded. I thought: how somber we are.

I was totally unprepared for the wild cowboys-and-Indians whoop she let out then. A war cry of joy, I hoped. She grabbed at me, yanked me by the collar, and pulled me to her. The fence cut into my stomach as we hugged. Her arms were strong and they hugged much harder than mine. I felt my hands clutching air behind her back and I knew my face had turned bright red.

I heard noises in her throat and she pulled away and put her hand to her chest. "Wait, let me recover. I don't know what reaction I'm going to have yet." The cat pranced away along the railing, ignoring me.

"Come on, get your car into the yard." She waved me forward and I got back in and drove along and parked in front of the house.

"Stand there a minute," she said as I got out. "Let me look."

The sun was in my eyes. I felt gawky as she studied me. I wanted to reach up to see if my hair was okay, to feel if I had any McDonald's French fries left around my mouth, but I didn't dare move, in case I broke the spell.

When she was through inspecting me, she took off her glove and very formally put out her hand to shake mine.

"How do you do, Michael Thorn."

"Fine," I said, noticing my hand was sweaty and shaky. "Fine, uh, Mother."

"Mother," she said in a voice as shaky as my hand. "That's me. Mother."

I followed her inside the house. She threw the jacket off and collapsed onto a sofa, her blue-jeaned legs sprawled out. She was wearing tan leather cowboy boots. I stared at the boots, afraid to look at her eyes again.

"I feel strange," she said. "Do you feel strange? It's going to be like that for a while. Right now I feel like a lump. What do you feel like?"

"A lump, too," I said, able to smile a little. I sat down on one of the chairs near the fireplace. It was a nice room. I was glad. It would be awful to find your mother living in a house you hated. It would be awful to find out your long-lost mother was into the kind of decor you thought was tacky.

"I need a drink," she said suddenly, jumping up. "How about you?" Then she stopped. "Are you old enough to drink?"

She poured out two small glasses of Amaretto. "Now you'll get the wrong idea," she said. I tried to protest, but she clinked glasses with me and said, "I bet you have a lot of wrong ideas anyway."

The Amaretto was sweet and burned my throat. "Don't gulp," she said. "Sip. We'll sit here and sip and get used to each other." She looked toward the door she had left open a little. "Puffin doesn't like you," she said. The cat was peering in. When it saw me looking at it, it ran away.

"I love cats," my mother said. "I had another one, Pushkin, but he got hit out on the road. I'm babbling, aren't I? God, I don't know what to say to you! I'm just glad. Glad it's all over."

It was fine with me if she was babbling, I didn't care. If she talked, I didn't have to say anything myself, and I felt the same as she did—I didn't know what to say, either. I was glad, too. I thought I should tell her that. I promised myself I would. Not right now, though. I took another sip of the Amaretto. It was making me feel warm.

If I were a normal-type visitor, she'd probably ask me about Rosie and Grandpop. But this wasn't normal. I wondered what I would be able to talk about when we stopped feeling like lumps. Maybe some subjects would be taboo.

After a while my mother looked at her empty glass. "It didn't work," she said. "I'm still shaking inside. I'm gonna show you some pictures now. You can ask questions and I'll give the answers and we'll have a conversation without any trouble at all."

She jumped up again and went off somewhere.

I sat in the room and felt a little scared that maybe my mother was a little nuts.

But slowly it all got better. She showed me pictures of herself when she was a teen-ager, standing in front of No. 5 Carhart Street. One had Grandpop sitting in a lawn chair. I couldn't believe it. He looked so much younger. There was a picture of her with me, although you wouldn't recognize me at all. I had a scrunched-up baby face. I looked like an old man. I was bald. I laughed and felt better, more relaxed. I almost made a joke about it: "If I looked like that as a baby, it's no wonder you got rid of me." But I stopped myself just in time.

I couldn't imagine the other pictures, I couldn't imagine it was her. Long kinked hair, crazy clothes, beads, moccasins, giants with beards standing all around. Love symbols, LOVE LOVE LOVE. She told me all about it, how she'd done the whole scene, including drugs.

"I was good when I was pregnant with you, though," she said. "I wanted a good baby."

Later, the sun sinks down behind the trees and the room gets chilly and dim. She lights the fire. She goes into the kitchen and makes us something to eat. Pours wine. She drinks a whole glass of wine, almost in one gulp. "Don't gulp," I tell her. "Sip."

She laughs. It's my first unlumpy remark. Some of the strangeness is gone.

"Remember that song about the world killing you?" she says as we sit in the big kitchen eating dinner. She hums a line off key. "No? Too young," she says. "Anyway, that was the way it was with me. The world always seemed to be killing me. I couldn't get it right, the way to survive like other people. Doesn't mean anything to you, does it? All from my yesterdays."

I thought she was probably a little drunk. Still, it was okay. She was probably not any crazier than a lot of people. Maybe she could be called eccentric. That was better. If you were eccentric, people thought you were interesting. If you were crazy, they got scared. I wasn't scared of my mother.

After dinner, when we were sitting in front of the fire, and owls were hooting outside and the cat Puffin had finally come in, I asked about my father. I figured it was time to ask, and I had a right to, since I had listened to everything during dinner. Everything had only been about her and now I wanted to know the rest.

"I don't know, are you ready for that? Is it necessary? Does it matter? You know, Michael, we both have the same father in a way. My father became your father."

"My real father," I said.

"Maybe someday. Not now. You can't have him, he will never be waiting for you at the end of a country road like I was. Do you understand that? It can never be. Your father is someone else now, with a life that has nothing to do with you."

"How can it have nothing to do with me," I asked, "when he's the reason I'm alive?"

I searched around in myself for some anger to

give my words more emphasis, and I was amazed that no anger was there. I'd had two glasses of wine with dinner and I was probably drunk, too. Rosie would be shocked. Mother and son get plastered at homecoming reunion. "Oh, why not?" I mumbled, thinking we deserved it on an occasion like this, but my mother thought I was still talking about my father and said I should trust her judgment.

"What happens when a traveler throws an apple core out of a car window and goes on his way? The seeds take root and an apple tree blooms. But the traveler never knows it. And the tree doesn't care."

"Huh?" I said. I felt tired. Tired or drunk, I don't know which. Both. "Doesn't matter," I said. "You don't have to tell me. I know who my father was. Johnny Appleseed."

"Tomorrow," my mother said, leading me upstairs and putting me to bed, "tomorrow we'll talk about you. You've heard enough about me."

She kissed my forehead. I heard her footsteps go away down the hall. Then I almost had a heart attack when something jumped on the end of my bed. Puffin walked on my stomach, settled down, and started to purr like an outboard motor. "You're not as quiet as a Mercedes," I told him.

I lay there as the room revolved like a carousel and I forced myself not to throw up. Finally, the room stopped turning and I fell asleep.

I dreamed of a masked man throwing an apple

out of a car window. The apple rolled along until it bumped into my mother. My mother smiled and the apple became a tree, and the tree bloomed and suddenly I was me.

27

Days run into nights run into days. I think I'll stay here forever. The idea of going back to Kornkill depresses me. Kornkill is where the nightmares are and I've escaped from them. I wish I could put the key in the ignition and tell the Mercedes to drive itself back to Grandpop.

My mother and I walk along country roads, with Puffin following us like a dog. She tells me about the basement apartment in Melford, where she lived when I was born. Grandpop used to bring us brown shopping bags full of groceries. But he was always angry. One day she told him not to come back anymore. After that we saw only Rosie. We met her on Sundays, when Rosie came out of church. My mother is amazed that I remember Rosie and the church. The tall spire. Rosie in her flowered dress and shiny stockings. My mother tells me Rosie always slipped her a five-dollar bill.

"What about my father?" I ask. My mother shakes her head and grabs at the long dry weeds at the side of the road, picking a bouquet of Queen Anne's lace.

"It was never the same after I was pregnant. He

didn't want to make it part of his life. We drifted apart." She hides her face behind the bouquet. "It seemed like everything changed between us after that night . . . that night. . . ." I know she means the night of my conception but doesn't want to say it.

I'm learning things about my mother. Like how she doesn't hug or touch very much. She avoids it. I think that's where I got it from, not wanting to kiss Rosie good-bye, feeling ashamed to say "I love you." I've been here three days and still haven't told my mother I'm glad, the way I promised myself I would. I'm relieved that my mother doesn't want to keep hugging or kissing me. We walk along the country roads, keeping a little distance between us.

Sometimes, there are long silences which I don't mind but which make my mother nervous to fill up. I don't follow everything she says, but slowly I'm putting the pieces of the puzzle together.

My mother and my father were having an affair that was wrong because he was married to someone else. They had secret meetings in restaurants and bars until one night she brought him to her apartment and made him stay over. He was angry the next morning, because he knew he shouldn't have done it. He was going to get in trouble with his wife. He told my mother he could never see her again, it was over. He drifted away as I started to grow inside her and she said having me was good because it made it easier on her heart.

"When you're nineteen, life is a dichotomy,"

she says. "You feel as tragic as death and yet you believe you're going to live forever."

And now I'm amazed that my mother understands such things. It's like she has been inside me and knows what I'm feeling.

But something troubles me. "If you hadn't got pregnant, maybe he wouldn't have left you," I say.

"No," she says, shaking the weedy bouquet to get Puffin away from a bird's nest. "He was always leaving me in his mind. He was the type of man who has lots of girls."

She keeps telling me we are going to talk about me. She wants to know everything. But we never get around to it. We might start in the morning, when she is brewing coffee and I sit in the kitchen window-seat and look out over the farm. It's a farm where nothing grows. My mother takes care of it for people who live in the city and don't want it to be vandalized. Maybe someday they'll want to come and reclaim it and send my mother away, but this doesn't worry her at all. She says that ever since she got out of the hospital, she only lives one day at a time. "I have faith," she says. "Things fall into place."

"Faith in God?" I ask, wondering if it is like Rosie, who puts everything in God's hands and says it's God's will if she saves sixty cents a pound on pork loin.

"Whoever's up there," my mother says, sweeping her hand across the air above her. "Whatever they call themselves."

Then she'll start asking questions. "So, how is

Rosie? Does she still darn socks?" But before I can begin to answer, she is telling me another memory, another story of her life, and my past is left untalked about for another day. Sometimes I feel like saying: "Mother! Do you want to know where I was for the past two years? Do you want to know that some people think I committed murder? Do you want to know that I sometimes wonder if I did myself?"

Inside me a voice warns not to push too hard. She isn't ready, doesn't want to know any bad things about me yet.

I am amazed that I have this ability to understand so well. Who are you? I ask the voice, because it is not the voice of the smirker who has haunted me since the school. The smirker seems to be lying low, hasn't breathed a word since I came to the farm.

The new voice, I realize, is only me, thinking to myself.

And so I feel like staying at the farm forever. I could plow the fields in the spring and we could make things grow. I could learn to live one day at a time, waking up to see if the sun is shining or if it's raining, deciding what to do. There are chores. We have to clear leaves and brush, prune bushes, mend the fence. We have to lay in a supply of wood for the winter and try to clean out the old chicken shed. It's a long building with a concrete floor and it stinks of chicken shit. My mother has ideas to make it into a painting studio. She used to paint psychedelic posters, she tells me. They're in a portfolio somewhere. Perhaps she'll find them and show me, she says vaguely. One of her paintings was used on the record jacket of a big rock star of the sixties. "I felt famous," my mother says. "It had my name right on the record album."

Maybe life would have gone on like this forever, I don't know. It's silly to believe in dreams. We were sitting out in front of the chicken shed, taking a rest after washing the place down with disinfectant. We were sunning our faces in the wintry sunshine, both of us smelling of Clorox, when we became aware of a man approaching the farm.

My mother squinted toward the road, shielding her eyes from the sun, brushing her long hair back from her face. I thought she looked very much like the girl I had seen that first day. I looked at the man, not really interested. People came to the farm once in a while, the mailman with a package, the milkman delivered milk and cream and eggs. He joked to my mother in the early morning, when I was still upstairs in bed, "When are you going to get your own cow, Miz Jones?"

The man loped along in white sneakers. He had a beard and was carrying a knapsack. "Shit!" I said, jumping up, knocking over a bucket of muck.

"What is it? Who is it?" my mother asked and I heard for the first time fear in her voice. She clutched at my leg, her strong fingers closing over my calf. I shook her off and ran to the fence, vaulted over it, and thudded down the rutted lane.

"Gary, you son of a bitch!"

He stopped and put his knapsack down.

Mopped his face with the back of his hand. "Hey, Mike. How goes it?" Like it was the most natural thing in the world.

"What are you doing here? Come to snoop out more research for your book? Interview with murderer's mother?"

"Aw, come on," Gary said. "Why don't you stop spouting off your big mouth for a minute and let me explain."

I looked back at the chicken shed. My mother was hunched, precariously, as if poised for flight. "It's okay" I called to her. "I'll be there in a minute." She nodded and disappeared into the shed. She'd been so calm the day I came, as if she had nothing in the world to be afraid of. I had made waves in the safe pool of her sequestered world. I hoped she didn't feel betrayed.

"Let's talk here," I said to Gary. He shrugged and sat down on the grassy edge of the track, groaning and stretching his legs. "Feels good to take a load off," he said.

I looked around. "Where's your car?"

"Didn't bring it," he said, giving a sly smile. "Took a train, a bus, and got a ride from some yokel with a truck full of used bathtubs. I've been walking the last few miles." When I didn't respond to his big saga he asked, "Want to know why?"

"You asked me to shut my big mouth. I'm waiting for you to explain."

He made the Gary gesture with his hands, shaking away my animosity. "I came to save your ass, that's what. I'm gonna drive back home with you so you won't be ambushed by Charlie Melville's posse."

"Who says I'm going home?"

"Oh ho ho," Gary said. "I have news. Developments. But even if you no longer give a shit for the great Kornkill murder, you have to come back. A mean honcho, Peter Barnes, is waiting for you."

"I don't know any Peter Barnes."

"That's the point. You were supposed to meet last month."

P. K. Barnes, the caseworker. I was supposed to make an appointment. All the rotten feelings I'd thought I'd left behind cascaded back into my stomach. "I'm in trouble?" I asked, sitting down next to Gary on the grass.

"Maybe I exaggerated, he's not such a bad dude. But it would be better if you showed. Not so good, driving without a license, no insurance, even if your grandfather tries to cover up. And Melville hasn't seen you around for a while, he's getting curious. You think I'm an insensitive son of a bitch, but I didn't forget what you said that night, about cops trying to catch you out."

"What are you, my guardian angel? How come you know so much?"

"In my position I have my ear to the ground. But like I said, you think I'm a shit, so there's no sense reminding you I said I was your friend."

"Oh, sure," I said. I moved away from him. "You're unbelievable, Gary. Rosie and my grandfather lied to me, but they did it for what they thought were good reasons, to help me. They really believed that. But you, you lied just so you could make money on your book. You used me."

"It wasn't to make money," Gary said. "I wanted to do something great. I wanted to make a statement that people would pay attention to. Okay, I was underhanded, it's true. But I believed Kline's theory. What's the difference between your grandparents believing and me believing?"

"Plenty," I said.

"You don't make a lot of money writing books," Gary said in a voice I hadn't heard before. It sounded sincere, but I had to watch out for his tricks. "I just wanted to write something good. You know what? I'll tell you something I never told anyone before. I avoid reading book reviews because I get upset. All those writers are writing stuff that people say is great, and I have to keep struggling. It's a shitty life."

"Tell me about it," I said. I felt a little embarrassed by Gary's confessions. He didn't look so know-it-all pushy anymore, sitting there on the grass with his legs sticking out in front of him. His beard looked ratty.

"I want to make it up to you, Mike. I found out a lot of things once I started looking from the opposite point of view. In fact, I'm gonna make that the motif for the book. I've got this theory—"

"My mother doesn't know anything about the murder or where I've been," I said, cutting him off.

"Don't you mention it. And don't you dare tell her about your book."

"Sure, anything you say," Gary agreed, but he looked disappointed and I knew he had been hoping for a juicy interview.

I knew then I had to go back. Gary's presence had broken the spell. He was like the wicked witch in those fairy tales Rosie used to read me, sticking a warty nose in to spoil everything—or in this case, a ratty beard.

I guess I'd known all along that it couldn't last. Probably my mother and I would have gotten on each other's nerves. She would have started acting like a typical mother and I would have acted like a typical son. She might even have been horrified to learn I had been a juvenile delinquent. And eventually I wouldn't find her eccentricity so interesting anymore. Maybe this way we could stay friends. Friends was about all I could hope for. I had to remember that.

So I took Gary to the shed and introduced him as my buddy from Kornkill. I explained how I had applied for a job and now there was an opening and I had to go back for it. My mother looked pale and relieved. Maybe relieved that Gary wasn't a threat. Maybe relieved I was going. It didn't seem to occur to her to ask why he hadn't just phoned.

"But you stay overnight, at least," she said. "Come on in the house. We'll have a drink. I'll make us dinner."

"My mother acts a little eccentric sometimes," I

explained to Gary as I showed him where he could wash up. "But she's not crazy."

"She looks all right to me," he said in a cocky way. I reminded him of what he'd promised—no interviews. "Okay, okay," he said.

She made it a big thing, lighting the fire and serving drinks, and setting the table with candles and flowers and cloth napkins. "A farewell dinner," she said, "but we can't be sad."

"I'm not going that far away," I said, but she didn't answer.

She brought out a bottle of wine and poured it into big balloony glasses. I took a few sips and put mine aside. It had given me a headache before. But Gary slugged his down and became friendlier than pie. I kept an eye on him, but he didn't slip up. Still, he was talking too much. My mother started telling her life story again and Gary was eating it up. I knew he was making mental notes even if he didn't have his notebook. I sat on the end of the sofa and felt like a third wheel.

"I was a wreck when I went into Amber Knoll," she was telling him, like it was every day you spilled the beans about being in a nuthouse. "I couldn't face life at all. I think these days, they call it agoraphobia and people take Valium and go to support groups. But in 1969 I was just a kook. Burned-out druggie, they figured, and maybe they were right. When they took Michael away I started using some hard stuff."

"Why did you let them take me away?" I asked

from my island on the sofa. I felt as if my voice had to travel a thousand miles to get their attention.

"I was a lousy mother," she said, and I couldn't tell whether she was joking or not. She and Gary laughed a little and slugged down some more wine.

I'm glad I'm leaving, I thought, if this is the way you really are. I took a slug of wine myself. And then I felt sorry. She was just putting on an act. How else do you talk about your pain to a stranger except by pretending it never hurt at all?

She went to check on the dinner and I glared at Gary. He was oblivious. I was about to tell him to cool it a little when my mother came back.

"What about Grandpop?" I asked, before Gary could horn in. "Don't you want to see him again?"

My mother stared into the fire. "No," she said after a time. "I don't. He knew where I was all those years and he never called, never wrote, he never once came to see me. First I hated him, then I felt anguished he didn't love me, then I just stopped caring. But Rosie. Sometimes, I feel bad about Rosie. She tried."

"Grandpop never visited me, either," I said, knowing exactly how she felt. Too late I realized what I had said. Gary covered up, asking about Amber Knoll in his reporter-type voice.

"I wasn't a patient all that time," my mother said, as if realizing she should clear it up. "I was discharged and then I went back and took a job. I guess it was a security thing, because the job wasn't what you'd call a career step. I got to wash bedpans and wipe dirty behinds. In a way it was comforting. I used to think I was doing a penance, until I straightened out my mind and stopped thinking such crap."

By the time dinner was ready, Gary and my mother were feeling no pain. I was disgusted with them and mad at myself for being such a drag. Rosie had been a stronger influence on me than my mother's genes. Thanks a lot, Rosie, you turned me into a prude.

Gary and my mother were talking a mile a minute. I started to pass the serving dishes around, so we could eat and maybe they would shut up. Finally, my mother remembered who I was. She looked at me across the table, a little cockeyed, I thought.

"We hardly had a chance to get to know each other, did we, Michael?" she asked in a drippy way. "Tell me, do you have a girl back home?"

Ugh. "I did," I said. "But we broke up." I wasn't telling about Mary Ann. I didn't need Gary knowing about that.

"Who was it? Someone from Kornkill?"

"Nobody you'd know."

"Oh, I remember lots of the people there. You get to know everybody in a hick town like Kornkill." She and Gary laughed.

"Lindsay Johnson," I said.

"Johnson," my mother said. "What family is that?"

"The Johnson family," I said. My mother sure was drunk.

She made an impatient gesture with her fork,

dropping pasta on the tablecloth. "I mean, which Johnsons? What are her parents' names?"

I don't know why she was getting herself worked up. But I didn't want a scene. Gary would put the whole scene in his book, I knew.

"Iraleen and Boyd. Except everybody calls him Johnny. They live a couple of blocks away—"

"I know them," my mother snapped. What the heck was she mad for? I was only answering the question.

Then she started talking to Gary about how she was going to fix up the shed for a painting studio and she seemed to get a little hysterical. I think even Gary noticed. He became very solicitous all of a sudden. "Here, let me help you with that, Mrs. Jones," he said. He took the dirty plates to the sink. My mother whipped cream for an apple cobbler for dessert. The beater slipped and the cream spattered the walls.

But by the time the cobblers were on the table and the coffee was ready, she had calmed down.

"Look," she said, holding her coffee cup with two hands, as if she needed warmth. "I'd appreciate it if you two wouldn't mention me in Kornkill. I want privacy. That might seem strange to you, Mr. Longman. You know I haven't seen Michael for years. I don't mind that he knows where I am, but I'd prefer nobody else did."

"I understand, I understand," Gary said. "You can rely on us."

"I won't say anything," I mumbled. Who'd be

interested anyway? But I wanted to know, was I supposed to go on pretending she was dead?

"And you're not seeing that Johnson girl anymore?" my mother asked me.

"I said I wasn't."

"I never liked that family," she said. "A lot of bad blood. It's just as well you don't get mixed up with them."

"Cripes, I wasn't going to marry her!"

My mother jumped a little at my voice. "Sorry," I said.

"No, I'm sorry. I shouldn't be sticking my nose in your affairs." She gave a wry smile at the word and I smiled back.

"It's all right."

My mother blew the candles out and switched on the overhead light and we all looked beat. There were circles under Gary's eyes. He said he was ready to crash and my mother apologized that he'd have to sleep on the couch.

I went to the room upstairs and Puffin followed me. I got into bed without brushing my teeth. Puffin walked on my stomach and settled down. I was drifting off into sleep, surprised I wasn't feeling so bad about going back to Kornkill, when I heard someone at the door. Gary? What could he want now?

But my mother's shape filled the doorway; she looked as pale as a ghost in her long robe. She was carrying a flashlight and she aimed it right at me, blinding my eyes.

"Ooops," she said, coming in to stand at the end of the bed.

"Michael, I'm sorry if this visit didn't turn out to be all you hoped it would be."

"It was fine, really," I said.

"I don't want you to be hard on Rosie. I want you to look upon Rosie as your mother, because that's what she was."

"But . . ." I started to protest.

"Just because I bore you, just because I'm your biological mother, doesn't mean there's anything special between us now. I know you don't agree with me, but someday you'll understand. Rosie did all the things I should have been doing. You trust Rosie, you rely on her, she won't do you wrong."

"Rosie's a little old-fashioned," I said lamely, still wanting to get my protest into words.

"Maybe so," my mother said. "But who knows how I would have turned out!" She said it in a giggly sort of way, and I had to laugh, too. She smacked me on the feet, maybe her way of giving me a hug. "Puffin's gonna miss you," she said. "Good night."

"Good night."

And then she was back again and her voice was urgent. "And you're not going to get serious about Lindsay Johnson, right?"

"What's the big deal?" I said, sitting up and dumping Puffin on the floor. "I already told you it's over."

"Okay. I just . . . well, I guess I do have some motherly feelings. I want you to meet a nice girl."

"Lindsay was nice," I said. *Was* was the right word. "Look, if it makes you feel any better, I have a girl friend. Her name is Mary Ann Hlavadic. I didn't mention her at dinner because I don't want Gary ribbing me about it."

"Hlavadic, Hlavadic," my mother was saying. "I don't recognize the name." She sounded ecstatic. "I'm so glad," she said, shining the flashlight in my eyes again.

I put the pillow over my head. "I'm glad you're glad," I said. "But what have you got against the Johnsons?"

"I went to school with them," my mother said, as if that was a perfectly logical answer. "Sleep tight," she said, almost sounding like Rosie.

My mother was a little dotty, I thought. She was terrified of the Johnsons.

28

"You still into this?" Gary said when we got into the Mercedes and he found *Thus Spake Zarathustra* on the seat.

"Not anymore," I said. Nietzsche didn't scare me. I'd walked over the abyss into the past. I'd looked back and it wasn't so bad. Gary tossed the book over the seat. I drove down the farm lane and out onto the road. I took one last look at the farm. Everything was quiet, still. My mother hadn't come to the door to wave us off the way Rosie would.

"Looks like snow," Gary said. "Let's make tracks."

As I drove, he told me the developments.

"Nothing to piece into recognizable form yet," he said, "but very important stuff. I went up to your house to get my stereo and I had a very interesting conversation with your grandfather."

"What happened to Suds?"

"We'll get to Suds later; he's interesting, too. But he wouldn't pack up my stuff for me. Anyway, I arrived just when your grandfather was going to take his walk and, very friendly, he asked me to join him. So we walked along that same path and he told

me it went to the graveyard where you used to work
for Linny Pollard. And I immediately thought about
you getting bopped on the head, so I asked him if he
ever walked all the way to the cemetery and he said
no, he had no interest in visiting the dead. He said
he might give up walking on that path because it was
getting too crowded. Since I didn't see anybody but
the two of us, I asked him to explain and he said
what with the beer cans and the cigarette butts and
the joggers, he was fed up. In fact, a few weeks
before he was almost run down by a jogger, a
woman he was acquainted with who didn't even stop
to say hello. I asked him to think a little harder just
exactly when it was and it turned out to be the same
day you got hit on the head. And"—Gary paused,
building up to his crescendo—"the woman was
none other than Iraleen Johnson."

Iraleen? Hitting me on the head and running
away? I could understand why Aunt Heva wouldn't
want to tell. But what was it Iraleen had against me?
What was so bad about me dating her daughter that
she had to slug me for it?

"Next," Gary said, "you'll be interested to
know that Iraleen is very chummy with a certain
Joanne who works at the post office. It's just conjec-
ture, but I got to thinking how those letters of Lindsay's might have been intercepted quite nicely if one
had connections at the P.O."

Gary could see I was excited, and he puffed up
like a big cat that had swallowed a couple of
canaries.

"Of course it's a serious crime, tampering with the U.S. mail," Gary said. "Iraleen must have been desperate."

"I have to admit, it adds up," I said. "Iraleen didn't want Lindsay getting involved with me and she sure put a stop to it. Maybe she followed Lindsay up to the cemetery that afternoon and saw us together. Lindsay said her mother was going off the deep end. It all seems logical. It solves the mystery of what happened to Lindsay's letters, and it solves the mystery of who hit me on the head. But what she has against me, I don't know. I guess she's just crazy, like Lindsay says."

"Well, if you'll excuse the bluntness, a mother could be worried about her daughter writing to a guy in trouble with the law."

"She could have killed me that day."

"Who can fathom the depths of a mother's wrath?"

"Oh, stop it," I said. "What else do you have? Is that all?"

"No no no," Gary said. "I've saved the best for last. I was talking to Suds and I found out something interesting about that night in Monrovia Park, just by chance. Now Suds, he's a difficult character. He wasn't too keen on talking to me, but when he found out I was writing a book, he changed his mind."

"Sure," I said. "I bet you conned him into thinking he'd be in it."

Gary looked sheepish. "Never mind that. He told me he took a fare to the park that night, and the time frame fits. I asked him how come he never came forward with this evidence and he said, 'Nobody asked me.' " Gary chuckled but my hands were gripping the steering wheel so hard, the knuckles were white.

"Go on," I said.

"The fare he took to the park was some young guy who acted strange, Suds says stoned, but that's Suds's catch-all for anyone he thinks is odd. Anyway, Suds left him off at the south gate, which is pretty dark and lonely. I got to thinking. Who was this person, what was he doing there, and how come nobody else saw him? Except maybe you. Think, Mike, does it ring a bell? Suds says the guy was wearing blue jeans and some kind of rain parka with a hood. Slight build, dark hair, dark eyes."

"A guy who had a date with the girl?"

"Could be. Probably they had a fight and he gave her a shove. You just happened to come along at the wrong moment."

I broke into a sweat. All this time I had been saying I saw a man and nobody believed me. The man was a figment of my imagination, they insisted. And as long as nobody believed me, he remained in my imagination, even though I knew he had been real. But now. Now Gary was handing me concrete evidence that the man existed. And it was terrifying to have him suddenly become flesh and blood.

"Gary, you weren't following me the night before I left, were you? Spying on me in a car with a girl out on the point?"

"Of course not. I was busy finding out your mother's whereabouts for you."

"This is important. You're telling the truth?"

He threw up his hands in his exasperated gesture. "Am I on your side? Am I breaking my butt getting evidence? Am I telling the truth?"

"Okay. The reason I asked is because *somebody* was spying on me. Somebody might be after me. Maybe the guy Suds took to the park."

"Maybe Iraleen again. Were you necking with Lindsay?"

"No! No, I don't buy Iraleen this time."

"What we need is a private eye," Gary said. "Or the police. We could find out if Iraleen had an alibi the night you were on the point."

"That's a little farfetched. I can just see Charlie Melville trying to help me."

Gary lapsed into a morose silence, maybe plotting how he could find a private eye. I kept my eyes on the road. It was beginning to snow. A shower of white flurries melted on the windshield. I turned the wipers on.

We stopped for gas and got some hamburgers. By the time we were back on the road, it was really coming down.

"This buggy got snows?" Gary asked.

"I doubt it."

Gary didn't seem worried; he fell asleep. I drove slowly, just hoping I'd get the car back to Grandpop in one piece. We were almost there.

"Hey, Gary," I said.

"Huh?" he said, waking up.

"How come you changed your mind about me?"

Gary considered. He looked out the window and noticed familiar landmarks. He began straightening his clothes, brushing at his hair in preparation for arriving home.

"You just didn't seem the type," he said at last. "Not very scientific or anything. Truth is, kid, I took a liking to you. But the real reason is Kline."

"Don't tell me *he* changed his mind."

"Nope. But he cheated me out of fifty bucks in a poker game and then tried to tell me I had a guilt problem. I figured he had to be a lousy psychiatrist. I never had a guilt problem in my life."

Truer words were never spoken, I thought, as we pulled off the parkway and made our way into Kornkill.

29

I was wrong about Nietzsche. He was smarter than me. I thought I had it all sewn up. Going back into the past, finding my mother, crossing the abyss without a scratch.

When I got home there were a few moments of uninhibited homecoming joy until the awkwardness of what I could or couldn't say about my mother fell like a cloud over us. Grandpop's eyes were wary, maybe even a little scared. He didn't really want to know.

Gary had come in with me, but he sensed the atmosphere and said he'd better get going before the roads got worse. He was staying at the motel at the other end of town. For the first time he didn't seem to want to gloat on succulent facts for his book. Still, I had to be fair, say thank you. He had uncovered a lot of facts for me.

"Don't forget to call Barnes," he said as he left. I promised I would.

Then Rosie, Grandpop, and I were left standing in the hall, looking at each other, until Rosie bustled to life and said, "I'll make some coffee. You must be cold."

It felt like déjà vu as we sat at the kitchen table, so much like that first day I had come home. Grandpop was being friendly.

"I see you brought her back without a scratch," he said, talking about the Mercedes.

"Yeah," I said. Then I forced myself to come out of the lethargy which was threatening to sink in. This was the same situation I'd goofed the last time, when Grandpop had tried to make a bridge. So I drank some coffee and told him how well the car handled on the road and how great it was to drive. I said I'd be getting my license soon and maybe, if he would let me, I could drive Rosie over to the mall. Rosie's face broke into a smile. Grandpop pretended to consider, looking serious, but I knew he didn't mind.

"Yep, she's a good car," he said, "there's nothing else like her." He told a story then, of the first time he'd driven a car. He was doing thirty miles an hour and got a ticket because the speed limit was only twenty-five.

"What do you think of that?" he asked. "I was a real hot rod in those days! I had a Stutz."

I couldn't get over it. Grandpop telling me a story. I thought of how he looked in my mother's photograph album. I would have liked to tell him. Maybe someday we could talk about the real things on our minds.

Things didn't change overnight, of course. Grandpop got tired and went away to his room. But this time he didn't tell me to go to bed.

As soon as he was gone, Rosie said excitedly, "Tell me, Mickey, how is Allie? Tell me all."

So I told her the best I could, leaving out the stuff about drinking so much wine, and telling me about having an affair, and acting crazy about the Johnsons. I said my mother was happy on the farm, and she just wanted to be alone for a while.

"Did she say anything? Did she give you any message for me?" Rosie asked. I was going to say no, because my mother hadn't given me any special wishes to take back, but then I remembered her saying: "Rosie tried. I want you to look upon Rosie as your mother." So I lied and said, "She said to give you her love." It wasn't such a bad lie.

Tears ran down Rosie's cheeks. She hid behind a coffee-stained paper napkin. "It's nothing," she said to me. "I'm glad Allie has found some happiness at last."

"I don't know," I said, afraid I had lied too much. "I don't know if she's happy. She seems sort of just there. Like she's not too worried about anything anymore."

"Some people call that happiness," Rosie said, wiping her eyes.

In the middle of the night I heard Rosie and Grandpop talking. I couldn't make out the words, just the sounds. I wondered if they were talking about my mother. And then the sounds drifted off and it was quiet.

I opened my window and looked out. The moon was up and the air smelled of snow. I heard the train whistle wailing a long way off. And I thought: What is there to hold you in Kornkill now?

I could straighten it out with P. K. Barnes, I could leave and go somewhere else. Did I have to stick around just to find the man in the park? Thinking about it, looking at the newly fallen snow glistening out on Carhart Street, it all seemed like a silly kid's idea.

And then I thought: It would always haunt me. I'd never be free of Kornkill until I knew.

And Nietzsche was probably laughing. Because I still had to make another trip across the abyss. And this was probably the dangerous one he was talking about. The dangerous looking-back. Because a man out there might just be planning to kill me.

I fell asleep with the light on. It woke me just at dawn, and I snapped it off and turned over. I'd been dreaming about something my mother said. It was important but I couldn't remember what it was.

In the morning Rosie showed me a letter.

"It didn't come in the mail," she said, puzzled. "It has no stamp." She was turning it over and over in her hands.

I thought it was a love note from Mary Ann. I'd called to tell her I was back. We'd meet tonight and talk. I reached for the envelope. It was addressed to me, but Rosie was right, there was no stamp, no postmark. I opened it up.

A thin white sheet fell out.

Want the truth? Meet me tonight at the wall. Midnight.

Printed with a pencil.

The snow, I thought. I yanked at the front door and saw marks on the porch. But the steps and walk were pristine. The snow was still falling. The vague footprints on the porch told me nothing. Except that someone had come to slip the letter through the slot. When? In the dead of night or maybe early morning, when I woke up to turn off my lamp.

I could go to the police. Shove this into Charlie Melville's face and make him take notice. But I could see him laughing. Nothing to prove I didn't write it myself. Crazy Michael Thorn. Have to send him back up the river.

You've got to confront your nightmares before they go away. I had to go. Find out. Face the music. But I wished I was back in third grade and something like the sun would happen and I would know it was all right and I didn't have to pay the ransom.

"Michael, for God's sake, close that door!" Rosie yelled. I did. I leaned against it. I listened hard for some advice from the smirker, but it didn't come. The smirker was dead, had been killed somewhere on the road between Kornkill and Emmiston. Now it was only me, asking questions and giving myself the answers. I had to go.

30

This was like a dream that repeats itself over and over. Bad luck comes in threes. First Ginger McKee, then the girl from Melford, next me.

I was scared and there wasn't a thing I could do about it. Had told Mary Ann about the note. Told her to stay away. Made her promise. Wouldn't get into trouble, would be all right.

I pushed through the snow and my feet were freezing. What I needed was wheels. Wait for the note-writer in a nice warm car. But no way could I get the Mercedes on a night like this. They didn't even know I was out.

Used to be I worried about things like that, sneaking out at night. Now my status had changed. Grandpop and Rosie relying on me. Michael can do it, ask Michael to take care of it, Michael, come and read the fine print on this Medicare form. Michael was a big shot now, no more little Mickey Mouse. Michael had graduated to adult. Shit, who wanted to be adult? Better when you had big people to take care of you. Better when the way to get rid of night-mares was to call for Rosie and a drink of water in the middle of the night.

So here was big smart Michael going to his rendezvous in Monrovia Park. Had a twelve-inch crowbar in my pocket and it was weighing me down, making it even harder to walk. Hadn't been in Monrovia Park since that night two years ago. This was the end of the line.

By the time I got to the park gates, I was sweating. I opened my ski jacket and pulled my hat off. But in a few seconds I was cold again, the sweat freezing on my face.

I curled my fingers around the crowbar. It was ice cold. The wind swirled the snow in front of my eyes. I looked at the ground for tracks, to check if the man was already here. I don't know how they did it in the movies. I couldn't tell shit from looking at the snow.

The wall loomed up at me like a living thing. I remember I said so many times at the school: I am never going to Monrovia Park again. I used to have daymares about the wall, how I had to climb up and up and it never ended, and then when I finally reached the top I would start to fall. I played it, like a tape, over and over in my head when I was working in the laundry or the kitchen. Just before I crashed to the ground, before my bones would splinter into a million pieces, I would stop the dream. I'd shake myself or slam my fist into the wall. People thought I was having a fit. They steered clear.

But now here I was and I was going to walk to the top, and a shake or a crunched fist wasn't going to bring me back home. I started up the steps that were full of snow. I had to go slow, to find a foothold. Funny thing it would be if I fell down this side of the thing and broke my neck.

It occurred to me that I could check the steps for other footprints, but the theater arced out around me and I was too scared to look. I had enough trouble just trying to keep breathing. So I gritted my teeth and kept climbing. After a while I heard some horrible sounds. Like an animal whimpering, I thought, until I realized it was me. God.

You're a jerk, I told myself. You're a number-one prize ass. Acting like a baby. Snot nose. I tried to get myself worked up into a rage, but I needed the smirker and he wasn't here. I hated myself for being so scared. Hey, Kline, look at me now. I'm going back to the scene of the crime. Do you think I'm going to find myself?

Actually, the thought of Dr. Kline helped me get angry. Remembering all his pompous theories about how this man-in-the-park was all in my mind. If it were possible, I'd like to take the man for a visit to Dr. Kline, wherever he was, cheating at poker somewhere. I'd like to shove the man up Dr. Kline's nose.

I reached the top and my worst fears came true. Somebody was already there, waiting for me. Dark in the shadows, dark against the snow. I blinked snowflakes off my eyes. Had the crowbar gripped in my hand.

He was wearing a hooded jacket. Hard to see his face. Came toward me, stepping slowly, like maybe he was afraid, too. The wind came whipping down, slugging at us as we stood at the top of the wall. The hood blew down. Long hair spiraled up like the tail of a twister.

"Iraleen." My lips were numb.

"I came to warn you," she said. "Johnny wants to kill you."

"No, get away," I said. "Get away if he's the one." I saw it all happening. Boyd Johnson jumping out of the dark, furious with Iraleen for her betrayal. He'd lash out at her, they'd struggle, and she'd go over the wall. Johnson disappearing into the night. Me, left facing a charge of murder.

"You can't stay here," I told her. "Go home. Get the police."

"I don't know why that man would want to harm you, do you?" Iraleen said in a perfectly normal, conversational voice. I might have been standing in her dining room, while she searched through the piles of stuff on her table, trying to find a recipe or picture of Lindsay to show me.

"My mother's flipping out," Lindsay had said.

"Iraleen can't control her heart," Aunt Heva had said.

Iraleen rushing down the path from the cemetery. Iraleen stealing Lindsay's letters.

Iraleen looking like a man until the wind snatched the hood from her head. Her hair was pulled back, tied in a ponytail. Her eyes were dark. She was wearing jeans.

"It was you," I said, and I realized I was using the same conversational tone.

"Michael," Iraleen sang, her voice like a lullaby. "Miiiiicalllll, you've got to understand." She was holding something in her hand.

I wasn't afraid anymore. I saw she was holding a knife, but I didn't have a drop of fear left. In fact, I felt like laughing. Dr. Kline had been right after all. There never was any man. I had only imagined him. All the time it had been Iraleen.

"Why?" I asked her. I kept my voice even.

"Johnny's girls," she said, stopping, looking confused. "He always had to have his girls. All the time, running around with girls."

Lindsay's father coming to the park to catch me and Lindsay . . . or Lindsay's father coming to the park to meet a girl who worked in an insurance company in Melford?

God, I could understand he didn't want to tell the police about his own wife, but why did he let it all fall on me? He could have said he'd seen a man. He could have said he'd seen some stoned guy and Suds would have backed him up.

"Iraleen, don't do this," I said. I had the crowbar in my hand, but I couldn't imagine hitting her.

"Michael," she said. "Have to do it because of you." The singing voice was scarier than the knife, which she was raising up as she came toward me. It was a big old kitchen-looking knife. Maybe it was dull. "Can't have Lin," she said. "Lin and you is a bad thing."

She was right in front of me. Her face was like a skull. I looked into her eyes and saw death waiting. She raised the knife and plunged it downward and I thought of *Psycho*, big knife, blood down the drain. I waited to feel the blood running down my flesh, feel the pain. But the knife just slid off my jacket and fell into the snow.

She got down on her knees, searching for it. I got down, too, but she got it first, picked it up by the blade, and hacked out at me blindly. I felt something sear my cheek.

I grabbed her arm, realized I'd dropped the crowbar. I kept thinking: This is Mrs. Johnson, Lindsay's mother, it's not polite.

She was strong. She wriggled out of my grasp. She had the knife again. She had the crowbar, too. What a dummy, I thought. She whacked me on the side of the head, and then I heard the bar clatter and thump away on the steps.

"Mrs. Johnson," I was saying, trying to be reasonable. Hadn't I heard you had to be reasonable with crazy people? "You don't have to worry about Lindsay and me. It's all over between us. I won't bother her anymore. I'll never see her again."

"A bad thing," she kept saying. "A dirty thing."

"No, Mrs. Johnson, you got it all wrong."

She was coming straight at me with the knife at waist level, propelling herself like a weapon. My ski jacket was open, it was heading for my stomach. Only one thing to do. I reached for it, grabbed the blade like I was shaking hands. It sliced into my palm, I could feel it hit the bone. With my other hand I pushed her back and she fell.

I threw the thing over the wall, watched it fall in the snowlight, stained dark with my blood, watched it disappear into the blackness. I didn't hear it hit bottom.

My blood was warm, running down into my sleeve.

"Nobody's going to believe you," she said. She pulled the hood back up over her hair. She edged away and got to her feet. "Nobody will believe what a kid from the nuthouse says."

"I don't care," I told her. I stuck my bleeding hand into the snow on the ledge and held it there. "It only matters that I know. I'll always know."

She looked hard at me and I was relieved the death had gone out of her eyes. She put her face close to mine, looked at me like she was trying to eat my soul. Then she gave me a little push.

"Johnny's boy," she said in a voice like a sneer.

She disappeared down the steps, as fast as the wind. It took me longer. I packed my hand with snow and stuffed it into my pocket. Every throb brought back the disgusting memory of that slithering blade. Yet, in a way, I felt fine. Maybe I could have whistled if my lips weren't turning blue. At the park gates I stopped to check if Charlie Melville's banana boat was waiting. But Monrovia Boulevard looked empty as far as I could see. The snow was coming down like a curtain and the streetlamps glowed like beacons from a fairy tale. I started to walk, hoping I would make it home.

Iraleen's words whispered through my veins. "Johnny's boy." It's okay, Mom, I thought, you don't have to worry anymore. Everything's out in the open now. Except that it has to remain a secret. I wouldn't feel bad at all, in fact I'm relieved, except I can't understand how he could hate me so much. What did I ever do to him except be born?

Up ahead I saw the red taillights of a car, the mist of exhaust. God, don't let it be Charlie.

Then someone was getting out, running toward me.

"Michael, Michael, what happened to you?"

I was safe in Mary Ann's arms.

31

Maybe everybody has to live with secrets, but I have enough to last me a lifetime.

I told Gary about Iraleen, but not quite everything. He assumes it was jealousy, that Iraleen got into a fight with a girl her husband was seeing on the side. He's got his murderer to write about now, although we both agree it could have been an accident. What I didn't tell Gary was about the other girl her husband was seeing on the side, eighteen years ago, the girl that was my mother. That's my secret.

"You want to make comments?" Gary asks me. "Look, they caused you a lot of trouble, these people. Iraleen letting you be implicated in the girl's death. Dr. Kline insinuating you were a murderer. What have you got to say about it? I'll put your comments in my book."

But I shake my head. The famous Michael Thorn has no comment. Those troubles were like the dreams the sandman brings, they grow in sleep and shadows. I was looking for the answers in the dreams. Now I'm awake and looking straight into the sandman's eyes.

I'll leave the writing to Gary. I hope he writes a

good book. And maybe if we all become famous, there won't be any secrets to keep anymore.

"You should be here," Gary says. "Don't you want to stick around to see justice done?" When he can't convince me, he throws up his hands and shrugs. "I hope you know what you're doing."

What I know is that I have to leave in order to survive. If I stay in Kornkill, I wouldn't have a chance. The horror would always be waiting for me around the next corner, like Charlie Melville's police car, waiting for an excuse to creep up next to me and open the door and say, "Get in."

"Okay, it's your decision," Gary says. "I hope you won't be sorry."

What I'm sorry about is that I never took Rosie to the shopping mall, or saw Wakefield again, and that I have to leave Mary Ann for a while. Mary Ann will have to wait for another time. Right now, I have to go away because Kornkill is eating me alive.

Because I could never again walk the streets without dreading that I'd meet up with *him*.

I remember him, one summer, sitting at the edge of the river where we used to swim even though it was polluted. Lindsay was telling me about dying, how Linny had put someone in a velvet-lined coffin.

"When I die, I want white velvet," she said in her little-kid voice. "Don't you, Mickey?"

And she told me what happens when you go into the ground: "The worms crawl in, the worms crawl out, they eat your guts and they spit them out."

I got scared. I ran away from her, up the rocky beach, to where he was sitting in his big hulking shoulders, his shirt off, the curly brown hair on his chest running with sweat.

"What's the matter?" he asked me, pulling me close. And I told him Lin said worms eat you when you die, and he threw back his head and laughed, put his big strong hands on my face.

"Hah!" he said. "Never mind those worms," and he gave me a big kiss, right on the mouth. And I felt like I would never be scared of anything again.

My father?

I don't believe it.

Me, Johnny's boy.

While my hand healed and Gary fixed it with P. K. Barnes to get me a job with Gary's old boss on the Cayuga *Post*, I felt numb. When the numb went away, I expected anger, but it didn't come.

The thing I realize is that everybody had a good reason for what they did. Some of them were altruistic and some of them were scared and some of them wanted to protect the ones they loved.

Gary had a good reason, too. He wanted to be a famous writer. In his own way he had helped me the most because he really wasn't trying to help at all.

Now the train comes down the track, hooting its lonesome whistle like it's glad to see me waiting on the platform. In the winter wind I smell the town:

Krackmayer's sausage factory and the brooding river and pine from the Monrovia Hills.

The train stops and a round, bulky conductor hops down, helps me with my suitcase when he sees my bandaged hand.

I take a seat next to the window. The train begins moving, we slowly creep away.

And yet it is like the town is disappearing and I am standing still. The sun licks the rooftops of the old and new buildings on Main Street. The red eye in the window of the Station Diner winks BUD once more, and then Kornkill, my home, is gone.

Home. That word. Your long-lost son, secret-slayer, says good-bye.

TWILIGHT™
WHERE DARKNESS BEGINS...

☐	1	**DEADLY SLEEP,** D. Cowan	91961-4-47	$2.50
☐	2	**THE POWER,** B. Haynes	97164-0-49	2.25
☐	3	**THE INITIATION,** R. Brunn	94047-8-23	2.50
☐	4	**FATAL ATTRACTION,** I. Howe	92496-0-31	1.95
☐	5	**BLINK OF THE MIND,** D.B. Francis	90496-X-35	2.25
☐	6	**VOICES IN THE DARK,** J. Haynes	99317-2-25	2.50
☐	7	**PLAY TO LIVE,** C. Veley	96950-6-56	1.95
☐	8	**BLOOD RED ROSES,** S. Armstrong	90314-9-19	1.95
☐	9	**DEMON TREE,** C. Daniel	92097-3-18	1.95
☐	10	**THE AVENGING SPIRIT,** E. Stevenson	90001-8-58	1.95
☐	11	**NIGHTMARE LAKE,** C. Laymon	95945-4-15	1.95
☐	12	**THE TWISTED ROOM,** J.P. Smith	98690-7-16	1.95
☐	13	**VICIOUS CIRCLE,** I. Howe	99318-0-24	2.50
☐	14	**FOOTPRINTS OF THE DEAD,** J. Callahan	92531-2-20	1.95
☐	15	**SPIRITS AND SPELLS,** B. Coville	98151-4-	2.50
☐	16	**DRAWING THE DEAD,** N. Selden	92141-4-22	1.95
☐	17	**STORM CHILD,** S. Netter	98289-8-21	1.95
☐	18	**WATERY GRAVE,** J. Trainor	99419-5-30	1.95
☐	19	**DANCE OF DEATH,** L. Kassem	91659-3-10	2.25
☐	20	**FAMILY CRYPT,** J. Trainor	92461-8-32	2.25
☐	21	**EVIL ON THE BAYOU,** R.T. Cusick	92431-6-39	2.25
☐	22	**THE HAUNTED DOLLHOUSE,** S. Blake	93643-8-15	2.25
☐	23	**THE WARNING,** A. Byron	99335-0-15	2.25
☐	24	**AMULET OF DOOM,** B. Coville	90119-7-32	2.50

At your local bookstore or use this handy coupon for ordering:

 DELL READERS SERVICE—DEPT. B1475A
6 REGENT ST., LIVINGSTON, N.J. 07039

Please send me the above title(s) I am enclosing $ _____ (please add 75¢ per copy to cover postage and handling) Send check or money order—no cash or CODs Please allow 3-4 weeks for shipment

Ms./Mrs./Mr _____

Address _____

City/State _____ Zip _____